Vampire Kisses 5

The Coffin Club

PRAISE FOR

Vampire Kisses

An ALA Quick Pick for Young Adult Readers
A New York Public Library Book for the Teen Age

"All in all, a good read for those who want a vampire love story without the gore." —*School Library Journal*

"As in her *Teenage Mermaid*, Schreiber adds some refreshing twists to genre archetypes and modern-day stereotypes." —*Publishers Weekly*

"Horror hooks such as a haunted mansion, a romantic teenage vampire, and a dark heroine who wins against the golden guys make this a title that readers will bite into with Goth gusto." —*The Bulletin of the Center for Children's Books*

"Schreiber uses a careful balance of humor, irony, pathos, and romance as she develops a plot that introduces the possibility of a real vampire." —ALA *Booklist*

Kissing Coffins
Vampire Kisses 2

"Raven is exactly the kind of girl a Goth can look up to."
—*Morbid Outlook* magazine

"Readers will love this funny novel with bite!" —*Wow* magazine

Vampireville
Vampire Kisses 3

"A fun, fast read for vampire fans."—*School Library Journal*

Dance with a Vampire
Vampire Kisses 4

"This novel, like the first three, is never short on laughs and shudders. Alexander is as romantic as ever, and Raven is still delightfully earthy. Schreiber again concocts a lively and suspenseful story that ends on a tantalizing cliffhanger. Fans of the series will be anxious to find out whether Raven's relationship with Alexander will survive."—*VOYA*

"A good choice for Goth lovers and fans of romantic vampire stories."—*School Library Journal*

Ellen Schreiber

Vampire Kisses 5

The Coffin Club

HARPER TEEN

Katherine Tegen Books

An Imprint of HarperCollins*Publishers*

HarperTeen is an imprint of HarperCollins Publishers.

Vampire Kisses 5: The Coffin Club
Copyright © 2008 by Ellen Schreiber
www.harperteen.com

Library of Congress Cataloging-in-Publication Data
Schreiber, Ellen.
Vampire kisses 5 : the Coffin Club / Ellen Schreiber.
p. cm.
"HarperTeen."
Summary: When goth-girl Raven follows her vampire boyfriend to Hipsterville,
she discovers a dangerous secret club inhabited by vampires who are feuding over
its leadership.
ISBN 978-0-06-128884-5 (trade bdg.) — ISBN 978-0-06-128885-2 (lib. bdg.)
[1. Vampires—Fiction. 2. Clubs—fiction.] I. Title. II. Title: Vampire kisses five.
III. Title: Coffin Club.
PZ7.S3787 Vame 2008   2007033823
[Fic]—dc22   CIP
                                                                          AC

Typography by Sasha Illingworth
1 2 3 4 5 6 7 8 9 10

First Edition

To my grandmothers—Sylvia Schreiber
and Ida Landsbaum
With all my love

CONTENTS

"Membership to our club comes at a very high price."
—Phoenix Slater

1

Bat Out of Hell

I flew from class like a bat out of hell.

Dullsville High's bell rang its final year-end ring and I was the first student to arrive at my locker. Normally the sound of the bell grated on my nerves like a woodpecker hammering on a sycamore, but this time the buzzing was as melodious as the sound of a harpsichord. It signaled one thing: summer vacation.

The two words rolled off my tongue like the sweet-tasting nectar of the blossoming honeysuckles. Aren't all vacations sweet? Given. However, summer vacation beats out its sister vacations—spring and winter break. Summer vacation surpasses them all with its incomparable advantages—two and a half months of freedom from textbooks, teachers, and torment. No detentions, lectures, or pop quizzes. No more spending an eight-hour day in the confines of Dullsville High, being the only goth in the preppy-filled school, or trying to lift an overslept pre-caffeinated head off my wooden desk. And most important, I could sleep in late. Just like a vampire.

My red and white school-colored handcuffs had been slipped off my wrists.

I was so pumped I even beat model student and my best friend, Becky, to her locker. It was the last time I'd have to remember, or forget, as I often did, the lock's random coordinates. Unreturned textbooks, notebooks, candy wrappers, and CDs filled the tiny metal closet. Forever the procrastinator, I waited until the final moment to clean it out. Unlike other lockers that had actual photographs of couples, staring back at me were oil-based pictures of me and Alexander that he'd painted and surprised me with, by hanging them in my locker. I gazed at them adoringly and carefully untacked one when I became distracted by the huge mess in front of me. I figured I needed a wheelbarrow to haul the load to Becky's truck but instead dragged out a dented garbage can and tossed out anything that I hadn't paid for.

"Summer's here! Can you believe it?" Becky said, catching up to me. We clasped hands and shrieked like we had just won tickets to a sold-out concert.

"It's finally here!" I exclaimed. "No more tardy slips or calls to my parents about dress codes."

Becky opened her locker, which had already been cleaned out. Photos of her and Matt presumably had been placed in a scrapbook with colorful captions, beautiful borders, and funky heart-shaped stickers. She examined the empty locker for anything else she might have forgotten.

"It looks like you even dusted it," I teased.

"This is going to be the best summer ever, Raven. This is the first summer we both will have boyfriends. To think, we'll be lying poolside with the hottest guys in Dullsville."

I spotted a painting of Alexander and me in front of Hatsy's Diner that still hung on the inside of my locker door. The stars twinkled above us and we were lit by the glow of the moon.

"Well, one of us will be," I said. And I wasn't referring to the fact that my boyfriend wouldn't be able to worship the sun.

I had a bigger problem—he wasn't even in Dullsville.

Becky must have read my wistful expression. "I bet Alexander will be back anytime now to have graveside picnics with you," Becky offered with a bright smile.

Alexander and his creepy-but-kind butler, Jameson, had driven the ailing tween vampire, Valentine Maxwell, to Hipsterville in hopes of reuniting him with his nefariously Draculine siblings, Jagger and Luna. After Valentine tried to sink his tiny fangs into my little brother, Billy Boy, my sibling and his best friend, Henry, began questioning his possible nocturnal identity. While Alexander was upstairs in his attic room saving the sickly boy with Jameson's Romanian concoctions, I figured out and confirmed Jagger's and Luna's location—the Coffin Club. And with that, Alexander was forced to leave me behind in Dulls-ville as he reunited Valentine with his older siblings.

Alexander had promised me that he would return to Dullsville shortly. However, what we thought would be an overnight visit to Hipsterville turned into two, then three days. Then longer.

The sultry homeschooled Romanian vampire Alexander had brought life into my already darkened one. As the lonely old Mansion remained empty of its unearthly inhabitants, I began to miss specific things about him—the way he softly brushed my hair away from my face or traced the lace of my skirt with his ghost white fingers. I missed his dreamy chocolate brown eyes, his bright, sexy smile, his tender lips pressed to mine.

I managed to remove myself as the third wheel from Matt and Becky's go-cart of fun. In the moonlit evenings, instead of reluctantly cheering on the school's soccer team, I often visited the empty Mansion, sitting beneath its skeletal trees, by its wrought-iron gates, or on its uneven weed-filled cracked cement front steps. Other times, I'd hang out in the gazebo where Alexander and I'd shared romantic desserts and stolen kisses.

I assured myself that at any moment I'd see the head-lights of Jameson's Mercedes beaming up the winding driveway, but every night I went home alone, the driveway devoid of any hearse-like vehicles.

I crossed each passing day off my Emily the Strange calendar with a giant black X. It was starting to look like a one-sided tic-tac-toe game. Occasionally the doorbell rang, and when it did, I'd race to the front door in wild expectation of Alexander wrapping his pale arms around me, scooping me up, and planting me with a passionate kiss. Instead of being greeted by my boyfriend, I was met by the Flower Power delivery woman holding a bouquet of roses. My already darkened bedroom was beginning to resemble Dullsville's funeral home.

With each passing day, I wondered what could be taking him so long. Was he once again protecting me from something dangerous and underworldly? My boyfriend, always shrouded in a bit of mystery, only made me love him more.

I had secured the painting of us in my backpack and then untacked a special item next to it—my Coffin Club barbed-wire bracelet.

The Coffin Club. The most gothically haunting nightspot in Hipsterville. I'd stumbled upon the hangout when I visited the funky town a few months ago. Unlike any other club I'd ever been to, the Coffin Club was the antithesis of Dullsville High. It was the first place where I really fit in, surrounded by similar taste, style, and attitude. I dreamed of returning there with Alexander on my arm. Only now I was miles away from my favorite nightclub and my favorite guy.

I untacked the painting of Alexander and me dancing at Dullsville's golf course.

I'd give anything to be rockin' with Alexander again. I imagined a painting that I could only fathom adding to my collection: one of Alexander and me dancing underneath the suspended deathly pale mannequins of the Coffin Club.

Just then Matt interrupted my daydream and gave Becky a peck on the neck—something I was desperately missing from Alexander.

Becky was right. I knew I'd see Alexander again—it was just a matter of when. But I was growing restless.

"I'd have thought you would have had that cleaned out days ago," Matt said. "Do you need help?"

"Thanks, but I want to savor this moment. I'll meet you guys out front."

As my favorite couple headed outside, a group of girls clutching designer purses and shoes passed by me like they were strutting down a catwalk, talking about European trips and boarding-school-style camps they'd be attending.

I just looked forward to the one place I *wouldn't* have to go—Dullsville High.

The warm summer air breezed through the open classroom doors and windows. I felt a few inches taller. I slung my backpack over my shoulder and briskly walked past the open classrooms.

I was just a few feet away from freedom. I reached out to push the main door open when someone jumped in front of me.

Nothing could spoil my mood today—not on my favorite day of the year. Well, almost nothing. Trevor Mitchell, lifelong nemesis and khaki-wearing thorn in my side, was staring down at me. "You didn't think I'd let you leave without saying good-bye?"

"Step aside before my boots make contact with your shins," I warned him.

"I haven't seen Monster Boy for weeks. Are you keeping him buried somewhere special?"

"Out of my way before I call the morgue. I think they have a vacancy."

"I'm really going to miss not seeing you every day." Trevor held his gaze a tad too long, like it had just hit him what he'd said. I could tell he was serious and it surprised him as much as it did me.

"I'm sure you'll get over it. You'll have your pick of uber-tanned *Baywatch* beauties to keep you busy."

"But what will *you* do? I heard Monster Boy left town. Forever. That will leave you in town all summer alone."

I hated that a rumor had started about Alexander being gone.

"He hasn't left . . . forever," I defended. "He's coming back. But it really doesn't matter because I'm going to see him. We're spending the summer together out of town and away from *you*."

I knew I was fibbing, but the thought of Trevor hanging out with lifeguards on each arm and mocking me while I waited alone at the Mansion made my mortal blood boil.

Trevor wasn't thwarted by my challenge. It only spurred him on.

"Then how about one kiss?" he said with a sexy grin. "Something to remember me by?" Though I had hints from Valentine of Trevor's inner desire for me, I was still suspect. I never knew what was going on in Trevor's head, much less his heart. I wasn't even sure he had one. Trevor was gorgeous—there was no doubt about it. His green melt-worthy eyes and his chiseled face could easily make him the next *Sports Illustrated* cover boy. But I was never sure if Trevor really liked me or just liked bullying me. Either way, he didn't move out of my way and instead leaned into me. There was only one guy I was going to kiss and that was Alexander.

I pushed my hand to his chest.

Trevor leered at me with a sexy grin. The more I fought back, the more he liked it. I was Trevor's ultimate soccer opponent and he was always desperate for one more game.

I paused for a moment and gazed up at the guy who'd tormented me since kindergarten. Trevor was really the only person who paid attention to me at school, besides Becky. I wasn't sure I wouldn't miss seeing him every day, too.

"I'll give you something to remember *me* by," I said. "The back of my head."

I pushed past him and escaped through the door to freedom.

I stepped out of Dullsville High and into the bright glare of the sun.

The year was behind me. Overall, it had been the best year of my life, for I'd met, dated, danced, and fallen in love with Alexander Sterling.

Students were walking home or getting into their daddies' overpriced luxury cars, heading off to begin their months of fun in the sun with people just like them. I'd spent a whole school year surrounded by people like Trevor.

My nemesis really forced me into seeing the light. It was time for me to be with people of my own kind. I wasn't going to spend my summer sans Alexander, much less another day.

There was only one thing keeping me and Alexander apart now. Me.

And that could easily be fixed with just a phone call.

2

Deadhead

More than a few months ago I'd waved good-bye to my mother at Dullsville's Greyhound bus stop and boarded the Hipsterville-bound bus to visit my ultra-conservative father's hippie sister, Aunt Libby.

Today I was on a Prozac high, minus the Prozac, ecstatic to return to the funky town of Hipsterville—home to unique coffee shops, with handmade coffee mugs and fresh scones (not the overincorporated cutout kinds with focus-group canned-in music), goth and hipster boutiques, and the perfectly morbid Coffin Club. I was excited to see Aunt Libby again, but even more important, I was only a few hours away from being reunited, or so I hoped, with my number-one vampire-mate.

I passed the bus ride doodling in my Olivia Outcast journal, imagining my reunion with Alexander. We'd meet inside the Coffin Club, where pale mannequins with bat wings hung from the ceiling and ghostlike fog permeated the air. Alexander would be waiting for me in the middle of the packed dance floor, with a single black rose. I'd run into his arms and he'd envelop me in them like a gothic Juliet. He'd lean into me and greet me with a long, seductive kiss, sending chills from my head to my combat boots. We'd dance the night away to the twisted sounds of the Skeletons until my legs could no longer hold me up. Alexander and I would venture off into a tiny church's graveyard, and we'd climb into a vacant crypt, where an empty coffin would be awaiting us. He'd close the lid on our night as dawn approached, and we'd snuggle together in darkness.

I was halfway through an episode of *The Munsters* on Billy Boy's borrowed (or rather bribed) iPod when I noticed the two-mile exit sign for Hipsterville.

Last time I arrived in Hipsterville, sunny skies and puffy blue clouds hung over the town. This time I was met with ominous clouds and a fierce downpour.

I covered myself with my skull-and-crossbones hoodie as the driver, undeterred by the pouring rain, unloaded suitcases from the bus's cargo hold. Finally I saw my suitcase, grabbed it, and huddled underneath the bus-stop shelter along with a crowd of other passengers. One thing hadn't changed—Aunt Libby was nowhere to be found.

I watched as each traveler was picked up by their party

until I was the only traveler left waiting at the stop. When tapping my boots in the rising puddles grew boring, I headed for the convenience store a few yards away. I checked the aisles for any hippie chicks with the scent of potpourri or women wearing Nairobi sandals and tie-dyed skirts. Unfortunately, all I saw were a few truckers and the hungry bus driver.

I grew more excited to see my hipster Aunt Libby again. She and I were outsiders among the Madison clan. My aunt lived an unconventional lifestyle, working as a waitress in a vegan restaurant to support her acting career. She was a free spirit, and Hipsterville was a funky town where she could be her organic-eating, hemp-wearing, liberal self. Though we had different tastes, I always felt bonded with her in that we shared a passion for being different.

Ten minutes later, Aunt Libby was still nowhere to be found. Perhaps she was stuck in a rehearsal or filling up the saltshakers at the restaurant. I could feel the glare of the tattooed cashier. I didn't want to appear to be loitering, which I was, or stealing, which I wasn't. My stomach started to growl. I hovered over the candy aisle, debating which sugary cavity-forming candy to buy, when I felt a tap on my shoulder. I turned around. A beautiful lady wearing pressed pants, a Happy Homes real estate jacket, and my dad's smile was standing in front of me.

"Aunt Libby?" I asked, confused.

"Raven! It's great to see you!" She gave me a hard squeeze and I could feel her rain-stained face against my own dampened one. "I hope I wasn't too late."

"I just got here," I fibbed.

"I bet you're starved. We can stop and grab a bite. I took the rest of the day off." She lifted my suitcase and we hurried into her vintage Beetle.

I couldn't help but stare at my aunt, who had traded her waitress outfit for a real estate one, as we buckled in.

"Surprised to see me in a suit?" she asked, obviously reading my thoughts.

"I don't think I've ever seen you without sandals and a flower in your hair," I teased.

"I figured it was time to get a real job," she confessed. "I didn't bother telling your father. I haven't been working that long and I've already taken a half day." She laughed. "So who knows how much longer it will last."

She started the car and the engine putt-putted as she motored through the historic downtown area.

Aunt Libby was such an independent spirit, I felt disappointed and sad that she was giving up her dream. I didn't want her to change, nor did I ever want to change. I wondered, if Aunt Libby had to give up her passions, would I have to, too?

"Have you given up acting?" I asked.

"No, it's in my blood," she said. "In fact, I'm doing a one-woman show. You can take the girl out of acting but not the acting out of the girl."

I felt relieved. "A one-woman show . . . That's great. Soon enough you'll have your own Oscar."

Aunt Libby chuckled, then turned serious. Raindrops pelted the windshield and the rustic wipers struggled to clear them as we headed toward her apartment.

Something felt strange as I gazed out the window. An eerie shadow blanketed the town as we drove through it. I thought I saw a few bats hovering over a church.

"Wow . . . Those look like . . ."

"Bats?"

"Yes."

"There was a nest of them in one of the houses we have on the market. You would have loved it!"

"Awesome."

"And you would have loved this house we just rented."

"Really? Is it spooky?"

"Completely. It was a half-dead manor house."

"A manor house?" I asked. It couldn't have been the one Alexander and Jameson had occupied last time I was here.

"Yes," my aunt replied.

"Well, there must be a lot in this town," I hinted.

"Not too many. And not one like this."

"What do you mean?"

"It had been abandoned for years. The back lawn was completely overgrown, and I think the floors needed to be rehabbed, but the new renter didn't seem to mind."

"Is it the one on Lennox Hill Road?"

"Yes. How would you know?"

"Uh . . . I remember seeing pictures of it in the paper the last time I was here," I lied.

"It does seem like a house you would love to live in. I wouldn't be surprised if it was haunted."

If someone had rented the manor house, then where were Alexander and Jameson staying? And how would I ever find them?

"Do you still have the key? Maybe they can give me a tour."

"No, the man who is renting it has the key."

"What does he look like?"

My aunt appeared puzzled.

"I was just wondering what kind of a man would rent a manor house. Perhaps a prince or a big-time executive," I prodded.

"This man wasn't a prince but more of a gentleman. He did look *creepy*—in the ghoulish sense of the word. I guess that's why he liked the house."

"Jameson!" I blurted out at the same time Aunt Libby tapped her horn and hit the brakes.

A sparrow quickly flew off in front of us.

"I brake for birds," she said with a smile.

I wondered why Jameson would rent the manor house. Did they plan on staying indefinitely? My heart sank. Then I remembered Alexander's reassuring words: "I will return soon." But what was keeping my boyfriend here?

We turned onto Aunt Libby's tree-lined urban street and she confidently, or foolishly, squeezed her Beetle into an anorexically small space between a truck and an orange scooter. Aunt Libby attached a lock to her steering wheel. She opened the entrance door to the 1940s row house apartment building, unlocked her mailbox, followed by her apartment door. Aunt Libby had as many keys as Dullsville High's janitor.

The smell of lavender incense bled through the cracks of Aunt Libby's apartment door before we entered. Once inside, a waft of floral scents hit me as if I'd just stepped into a flower conservatory.

Though Aunt Libby's attire had changed, her apartment decor hadn't. Besides a few stacks of real estate manuals sitting on her coffee table, the sixties and seventies still ruled the one-bedroom apartment. Beaded curtains hung from the frame of her bedroom door and half-melted candles lined every inch of available space, from the mantel to the floor.

As I shed my rain-soaked clothes for dry ones in Aunt Libby's dinky bathroom, I imagined what my life would be like on my own if I'd never met Alexander. Who would I grow up to become? Dullsville was way too dull for a girl like me. I'd probably end up in Hipsterville in an apartment similar to my aunt's, only it would have dripping wax candelabras, black lace curtains, and a gargoyle headboard on my bed.

But what would it mean if I couldn't share it with Alexander? Living on my own and working perhaps as a bartender at the Coffin Club night after night. I felt a pang of loneliness for my aunt—she had eaten, slept, lived by herself for as many years as I could remember. Instead of being dragged down by her independent lifestyle, Aunt Libby seemed to thrive on it. She serial dated and had a wide circle of friends from her theater community. Aunt Libby was gorgeous. Someone as hip and cool as she could get any man she wanted.

I reapplied my chocolate eye shadow and liner and towel dried my damp hair. I smelled teriyaki sauce and found Aunt Libby—the one I'd always known, wearing embroidered jeans and jeweled flip-flops, a halter top underneath a linen jacket—stir-frying in her wok.

I sighed, relieved that my aunt had returned to her inner Deadhead.

Aunt Libby served our healthy entrees. We sat down at her coffee table, on oversized mismatched fluffy pillows, surrounded by candles, incense, and a spicy Asian meal.

"I think I'm getting married!" she suddenly announced. "I've been dying to tell you."

"You are?" I asked, surprised. "Congrats! Dad didn't mention . . ."

"Well, okay, it's not official or anything. In fact, we haven't officially gone out yet. I just met him last night."

Aunt Libby's face flushed bright red. She grabbed a brown hobo purse that was sitting on her paisley futon and pulled out a rainbow-colored beaded wallet. She opened it and presented me with a Renegades paper napkin. It had a man's name and phone number written on it. "He has beautiful handwriting, doesn't he?"

"Devon. That's a cool name."

"I can't wait to tell you all about him."

"Tell me all!"

"He has pool-colored eyes and salt-and-pepper hair."

"He sounds dreamy."

"I noticed him in the audience when I was onstage. I

almost couldn't see him because he was just outside the glare of the spotlight. He has the most piercing blue eyes I've ever seen. Our eyes locked and I forgot my lines. I stood there, frozen, for what seemed like hours. He had this hypnotic stare."

I laughed. Aunt Libby was like a sixteen-year-old girl who had fallen in love.

"When the show was over, he was waiting for me. We had this intense connection I've never felt before."

"I know exactly what you mean. That's how I feel about Alexander. That's why I had to come here. . . ."

"Come here?" she asked.

"Uh . . . yes, for girl time."

"I know what you mean. I'm bursting at the seams to talk about him, but there's not much I know—besides how handsome he is!"

"I'm sure I'll be calling him Uncle Devon within a matter of days. Can I wear black to your wedding?"

"I wouldn't want it any other way. We have a date in the next few days and you have to come."

"You are going out on your first date with him and you're going to show up with me? Your vampire-obsessed niece? Even I don't think that's a good idea."

"You have to come. I can't wait for you to see him . . . and I can't leave you here alone."

"Of course you can. But we can talk about it tomorrow."

We had just placed the dishes in the sink when Aunt Libby noticed the time.

"I have a drumming class tonight. I was hoping you'd join me."

"Well . . . I . . ."

"I don't have to go."

"No, I don't want you to miss it on account of me."

"It's a master class tonight. Otherwise I wouldn't think about going."

"Please go. I'll be fine." I wouldn't be able to run across town and try to make contact with Alexander if I were stuck in a drumming class all night.

"Think about it while I get ready."

While Aunt Libby prepared for class, I stretched my legs out on her futon and turned on the nineteen-inch TV with a leaning cactus on it. Her TV received only local channels and the color faded in and out at will.

"How do you live without cable?" I asked, frustrated.

I switched on the local news. Normally I would have turned the set off quickly and kept myself busy text-messaging Becky about my arrival. But something caught my eye.

"Hi, I'm Anne Ramirez, reporting to you live. I'm standing with Fred Sears, a farm owner who discovered a crop circle in his wheat field. This is the second one reported in this county in less than a month, this one being a little more intricate than the last."

The camera panned to the wheat field, where stalks had been crushed against the ground in the shape of a fifty-foot circle, with several smaller circles in the center.

The petite woman stood next to the black-haired

farmer, who was three times her size. "When did you notice this?" she asked.

"When I woke up. It just 'cropped up,'" he joked.

I rolled my eyes as I watched two preteens running around it.

"I saw bats hovering over the area last night," said one boy, almost breathless, to the reporter.

"Those were crows, stupid," the other admonished. "Flying away from the alien spacecraft that landed here."

"They were bats!" the boy insisted.

"Anything interesting?" my aunt called from her room.

"Just a crop circle with hovering bats."

"The girls at the agency were talking about that at lunch. They are convinced it's all for publicity."

The video switched to an aerial shot from WBEZ's helicopter. The circle was impressive.

Then the camera was back on the reporter.

"Spacecraft or just spaced out? You decide. Back to you, Jay."

"That's so bogus . . . ," I called to my aunt. "I saw a report on TV once where kids confessed to creating them. They demonstrated to the reporter how in the middle of the night they used a stake, a rope, and wooden boards to press down the stalks and form a giant circle."

My aunt came back into the living room dressed in an off-the-shoulder cotton top and pea green yoga pants. "I believe we aren't the only ones in the solar system. They could be aliens. No one has disproved their existence."

"Are you kidding? You really believe in aliens?"

"Do you really believe in *vampires?*"

She had a point. "Yes, but they are real," I blurted out without thinking. "Uh . . . I mean, no one has disproved their existence."

"I'm just saying," Aunt Libby argued as she added some final touches to her hair, "it could be the markings of an alien aircraft—or a signal for other aliens. Aren't crop circles meant to be viewed from the air?"

"The boy on the news swore he saw bats last night. Maybe it could be vampires signaling other vampires," I suggested.

"Hmmm. I like your theory better. Aliens are kind of odd-looking and have green heads. Vampires are sexier. I'd prefer to see them invade our town."

I gave my thought pause as the anchor turned the focus to weather. "Our five-day forecast calls for rain and fog."

Curiosity getting the best of me, I couldn't shake the farm boy's claim. After all, who better to go undetected in the night than vampires? They could easily see the circles as they fly in bat form over the horizon. There was no way to confirm my theory by sitting in my aunt's apartment, and it wasn't like me to not poke around for some clues.

"Do you mind if I check my e-mail?" I asked.

"Sure. The computer is already on."

I searched the Internet on my aunt's iMac for vampires and crop circles. I scrolled past various movie and book sites until I came to a small website that specialized in paranormal sightings in North America. All the entries detailed unearthly bright lights, alien abductions, and hoaxes. Just as I began to click out of one such site, I spotted something of interest. Instead of green-headed monsters, one blogger claimed that the night before he spotted a crop circle, he'd seen a swarm of hovering bats.

I thought I'd stumbled onto something big. The entry had to be posted by a Harvard scholar, a scientist, or a Nobel Peace Prize winner. Instead it was signed Bob from Utah.

Bob could have been a crackpot like any other, a bored kid in study hall posting erroneous entries on websites, or, like me, a vampire-obsessed mortal with an overactive imagination. But I took his single entry as a sign.

There was one way to investigate my theory further. I had an advantage that Bob in Utah didn't—I was dating a vampire.

"Are you sure you don't want to come with me?" my aunt asked as she picked up an African drum lying next to the fireplace.

"I'm beat—no pun intended," I teased, shutting down the computer. "Do you mind if I just crash?"

Even if I wasn't preoccupied about reuniting with Alexander, the thought of amateur drummers learning how to bang on instruments for two hours was enough to make me mental.

"There's plenty of tofu patties in the fridge and soy pudding in the cabinet. I'll call you on your cell at break to check in."

"Thanks, Aunt Libby," I said, giving my dad's sister a

hug. "I really appreciate your letting me visit you again."

"Are you kidding? I love having a roommate. Just bolt the door behind me and don't buzz anyone in. And please, don't get abducted by aliens. Your father would kill me."

3

The Manor House

Once again I found myself waiting at a bus stop. This time I hung outside Aunt Libby's apartment in the drizzling rain anticipating the arrival of the number seven. I paced back and forth for what seemed like an eternity, waiting for it to turn down my aunt's street.

I had to admit I wasn't overly excited to be boarding another bus, having just ridden one for several hours, but it beat borrowing Aunt Libby's bike and cycling across town in the rain. It was imperative that I reach the manor house before sunset, otherwise Alexander might be out for the evening and my surprise reunion would be delayed.

Finally I saw a bus lumbering around the corner and almost cheered when I saw it displayed a yellow seven digitally. I shoved my money in the change receptacle and quickly grabbed the cold aluminum pole. Though the bus was half empty and many seats were vacant, I chose to stand for the duration of the ride. Having missed the Lennox Hill stop the last time, I refused to have anyone or anything blocking my view and further delay reaching Alexander. My heart beat faster with every stop and acceleration. I thought I'd caught a break since there weren't that many passengers on the bus, but twice as many were waiting to board the number seven at the next stop. After what felt like the span of summer break itself, I spotted Lennox Hill Road. I remembered that to notify the driver of my desire to disembark, I needed to pull on the white wire that ran above the windows. I repeatedly tugged on the cord like I was signaling an SOS.

"I heard you!" the driver shouted back.

The rain had ceased. I hurried up Lennox Hill Road, scurrying through puddles and jumping over slimy but cool earthworms.

Rain-soaked estates lined the street. The pristine grass lawns were drenched and several branches and leaves were scattered in the asphalt driveways.

Then, at the end of the cul-de-sac, plain as a stormy day, sat the monstrous manor house. The gruesome estate appeared to be even more overgrown and unkempt than the last time I'd visited it.

Steam seeped into the air, creating a spooky fog around the palatial home. Moss and wild vines overtook the house like a giant spiderweb. Stone gargoyles sitting upon the jagged wrought-iron gates seemed to smile at me as I approached. Sticking in the half-dead, weed-filled lawn was a Happy Homes sign. I hurried past the broken bird-bath and up the cracked rock path. My heart pounded as I reached the familiar arched wooden front door.

The dragon-shaped knocker that had fallen into my hand upon my first visit had not been replaced. Perhaps it was still hidden in the untamed bushes where I'd tossed it.

I knocked on the door.

I waited. And waited.

Jameson didn't respond. I pounded my hand against the door again. Still no response. Not even a torn curtain rustled.

I turned the rusty doorknob and pushed against the door, but it was bolted shut.

I raced through the soggy grass, past the servants' door to the back of the house. I darted up the few cracked cement stairs and eyed the back wooden arched door. There wasn't a bell to ring or a knocker to knock. I pounded my hand on the door. When no one answered, I looked around for another door.

I was becoming concerned that it wasn't Alexander and Jameson who had rented the place after all. There were no signs of my boyfriend or his butler's presence. I peeked in a basement window and it appeared to be in the same vacant state.

I spotted the tree I had once climbed to see into Alexander's room. I might have been able to confirm once again that he was inside, but climbing the rain-soaked tree was not a viable option.

I peered around the backyard to see if I saw Jameson's Mercedes. The cracked asphalt drive was vacant of cars. I saw a concrete bench and a wrought-iron arched trellis overrun with creeping vines. A circular rock bed where a pond must have once been was now filled with rainwater. I spotted a decaying one-car detached garage that appeared as though it might collapse with a gentle nudge. I headed straight for it. My heart raced as I darted toward the garage. I noticed a lock on the door. It was brand-new.

Though I was an expert at sneak-ins, I was lousy at picking locks. I'd need the help of Billy Boy's nerd-mate gadget whiz, Henry, but he was obviously miles away. The dilapidated garage was sturdier than it looked. With all my strength, I couldn't move any of the paint-chipped wooden boards.

I examined the outside of the garage. There wasn't a window on any side. I did notice a skinny crack between two boards about hip height from the ground on one side. Light from the setting sun illuminated the skinny space. With my best vision, I could barely make out a white sheet covering what must have been an old bike or lawn mower. And next to it, something sparkling in the light. On further inspection I noticed a Mercedes hood ornament.

I raced back to the manor house. I placed a discarded box underneath the kitchen window and stepped on it. I teetered on tiptoe, doing my best to see inside. The window was dusty, so it was almost impossible to see indoors. I tapped the glass pane relentlessly and peered through a hole the size of a quarter.

Suddenly a bulging eyeball gazed back at me.

Startled, I screamed and fell off the box, back onto my bottom in the wet grass.

I heard the sound of locks being unlocked and the door being opened.

I froze. What if I'd been wrong when I'd spotted a Mercedes ornament that I was so certain had belonged to Jameson? I was so excited to see it, I hadn't even considered my discovery. The stored car could have been any make or model, or white for all I knew. At any moment I would be caught trespassing, thrown in Hipsterville's juvie jail, or forced to return to Dullsville.

I bit my black lip and held my breath.

Then, at the screen door, Jameson appeared.

Alexander's butler struggled to see me through the glare of the mesh door.

"Jameson, it's me, Raven."

"Miss Raven?" he asked, confused. He opened the door. "It can't be you. What are you doing here? In the backyard?"

I jumped to my feet, dusted off my miniskirt, and raced up the uneven steps toward the Creepy Man. Jameson wrinkled his pale forehead.

"Miss Raven, I'm surprised to see you here. But pleasantly, I might add," he said with a skinny-toothed smile.

"I'm visiting my aunt Libby here in town," I said, relieved to see the bony butler. "I wanted to tell Alexander, but there wasn't a way to let him know. I seriously think it's time you and Alexander got cell phones."

"Please come in. It will be dark soon."

The smell of sweet potatoes filled the high ceilings of the rustic kitchen. Jameson was preparing dinner, or, in Alexander's case, breakfast.

"Will you be staying?" he asked in his thick Romanian accent.

"I'd love to, if it's not a problem."

"There is always room for you at our dinner table."

My heart melted at Jameson's kindness. I was dying to press the bony man for information on what they'd been doing in Hipsterville and why they had rented the manor house, but that would have to wait because there was something of more importance resting somewhere in the estate.

"Can I see Alexander?" I asked anxiously.

Jameson, wearing oversized brown oven mitts, opened the door of the old-fashioned oven and pulled out a tray of aluminum-foil-covered sweet potatoes. Behind him, the dirt-stained window stared at me like a hotel oil painting—poking through intermittent clouds was the setting sun.

"You know Alexander prefers to sleep during the day," he reminded me.

"Of course . . . I just thought . . ."

"Well, it is quite a surprise you have arrived," he said, politely entertaining me. "I'm sure Alexander will be very pleased you are here."

"I hope so! How long do you and Alexander plan to stay here?" I asked.

Jameson paused, then appeared distracted. "Did I set the table?" he wondered.

"I am sorry to drop in on you like this," I apologized. "Can I help you set it?"

"That won't be necessary, Miss Raven. Why don't you sit and relax in the study. Alexander will come down soon."

"May I take a quick peek around?"

"Of course, but stay on the first floor. I didn't have time to clean the other rooms today," he said.

If the first floor's appearance was Jameson's idea of cleaning, I could only imagine what the second floor was like. Dust balls clung to every corner, and cobwebs hung from the antique crystal chandeliers. The estate was far too grand for one creepy man to vacuum. The manor house was at least ten degrees colder than the Mansion and far emptier. The floorboards were uneven and watermarked. I wandered in the hallway; the walls were empty of portraits and the wallpaper was faded and patched with stains. All rooms and walls were bare, including what must have been a parlor and library. The only exception was the dining room, where a long rectangular stone table sat in the middle of the room, antique black velvet chairs at each end.

Jameson had warned me to remain on the first floor as if he were Glinda the good witch telling Dorothy to stay on the yellow brick road. From the foot of the grand staircase, I could only see a royal blue curtained window at the end of the first flight. I wondered what lay past the two flights out of view above me. Figuring I only had a moment before Jameson began setting the table, I crept up the once regal staircase. Like Dorothy, I betrayed the path.

Chills danced down my spine as I snuck through the narrow and lonely hallway. I opened door after door, revealing empty bedrooms and closets, my footsteps echoing in the cavernous and vacant space. Where the Mansion's rooms were filled with furniture, books, and antique mementos, the manor house's rooms were stripped of any memories. The only room that showed any sign of life was at the far end of the corridor. Its contents: a single bed and a cedar dresser. I presumed it was Jameson's living quarters.

When I softly shut the Creepy Man's bedroom door, I noticed something dangling in the hallway ceiling above me. A short, wiry piece of white rope hung from a square door overhead. It was out of arm's reach, but with a good jump I might have been able to grab it. I knew I should go back downstairs, but that went against my true nature.

The first time I jumped, I didn't even reach the cord. The second time, my fingers touched it. Finally, on the third try, I caught the cord between my fingers. With all my might, I quickly pulled the rope and snapped it securely in the palm of my hand. The door slowly creaked down toward me and a staircase folded out like a fire escape in a New York City alleyway. Surprisingly the wooden steps seemed to be in relatively good condition. Perhaps the former tenants didn't see the need for a darkened attic hideaway.

I quietly ascended the stairs, curious to examine what lay at the top. A glow from the second floor shone like a small spotlight, illuminating a portion of the attic. A musty smell filled the gymnasium-sized room. The attic, like the rooms below, appeared bare. Alexander's easel, art supplies, and mattress were nowhere to be found. A single ray of sunlight peeked through a circular window in the far end of the sloping attic walls. I tiptoed over and noticed an unpainted plain old oak armoire beneath the window. I tried to open its doors, only to discover they were locked. Perhaps the skeleton key was hiding in the attic somewhere with real skeletons. I glanced around, trying to adjust my vision in the darkness. It was then I saw something shrouded in the shadows—a black room divider. I crept over to the corner of the attic and peered behind the six-foot-tall wooden screen.

I could barely make out a night table and a pewter candlestick with a half-melted white candle. Behind it stood an easel with a covered painting, art supplies scattered beneath. Then I noticed something familiar on the nightstand staring back at me. It was the picture Alexander had painted of me and kept on his nightstand at the Mansion. There next to the tiny table was a single black coffin.

I was standing alongside my sleeping vampire boyfriend. I pressed my ear to the cold coffin lid. I could barely hear what I thought to be breathing. My heart raced with his every breath.

I knew the sun was setting because the cast of light from the attic window was slowly shrinking. It only took a few minutes for it to dwindle to the size of the nightstand. Finally it was as thin as a pencil, then it was gone.

A small amount of light still appeared from the open door in the attic floor. It took my eyes a moment to adjust to the new illumination.

Just then I heard someone stirring inside the coffin.

I stepped back, and the heel of my boot snagged against a tiny nail protruding from the bottom of the screen. For several moments, the room divider and I teetered back and forth. I was about to cause a major commotion. I regained my balance and managed to return the screen upright and steal myself behind it. I peered through a tiny crack between the ruler-sized boards, my heart racing even harder now.

The top of the coffin lid began to creak open ever so slowly toward me, leaving me unable to see inside until it reached a ninety-degree angle. I didn't see fingers, a hand, or anything opening it, nor could I make out anything—or anyone—behind it. I peeked around the screen.

It was then I saw a sleepy Alexander staring right at me.

Startled, I screamed.

He paused. His chocolate-colored eyes turned blood-red. "Raven!"

I tried to catch my breath and regain my composure. "I didn't mean to scare you—or myself," I apologized.

"What are you doing here?" he asked, shocked.

"I came to see you—"

Alexander stepped out of the coffin barefoot, wearing a black T-shirt and black boxers. He paused by the nightstand. He didn't run to me and scoop me up in his arms. It wasn't the reaction I'd expected.

"I thought you'd be glad to see me," I said. It took all my strength not to hug him.

"I am, it's just—" Alexander stood awkwardly. He fixed his hair with one hand and straightened out his clothes with the other.

"Are you upset I'm here?" I asked. "I couldn't wait another day."

"I just woke up," he said self-consciously, wiping one eye with the back of his hand. "I would have preferred a little warning." His stern demeanor then softened. He looked sexy, his long hair tousled and his clothes still askew. Even in the darkness Alexander lit up the room. A warm smile overcame his sleepy face.

"I missed you so much I couldn't breathe," I said, daring to run to him.

"Me too," he said, now gazing down at me. He brushed my hair away from my cheek, pulled me into him, and swept me up in his arms. I hugged him around his neck, and my black-fingernailed hands coursed through his silky black hair. He leaned into me and kissed me, passionately, like I'd dreamed about night after night since he left the Mansion. Alexander took my neck in his mouth, like a wolf would a swan. The sharp edge of his teeth slid against my skin, then he suddenly pulled back.

"Miss Raven? Miss Raven?" Jameson called from below.

Alexander let me down. His red eyes faded to their natural brown. He seemed shaken, but I held his hand reassuredly. I knew I was safe in his arms.

"She's up here with me, Jameson," Alexander answered.

"I thought she might have gotten lost. Dinner is ready."

"I was just on my appetizer," he whispered to me with a wink.

"Desserts are even better," I said, and gave him a quick kiss on the cheek.

I felt as tiny as a Polly Pocket doll in a Barbie Dream House as I sat alone at the limousine-length table in the stately and stark mile-high-ceilinged dining room. A black lace tablecloth was draped over the stone tabletop, and a single candelabra flickered as the centerpiece. The macabre table was set with Wedgwood china plates, sterling silver cutlery, and crystal goblets—everyday settings for my vampire boyfriend. The Madison family ate this fancy only once a year, when my grandmother dusted off her china and made Christmas dinner; otherwise it was strictly Pfaltzgraff.

My combat boots grazed the patched wooden floor as I anxiously swung them back and forth underneath the table, impatiently waiting for Alexander's entrance. I was hoping a ghost would float by to keep me company, but no specters arrived. Soon I sensed a familiar presence behind me, followed by hands caressing my shoulders.

I felt two lips press against my neck. I grew so hot I thought I'd melt the ice cubes in my crystal goblet. The ends of Alexander's midnight-colored hair were still damp from a quick shower and brushed against the back of my bare shoulder. He smelled heavenly with the sweet scents of Drakkar and Irish Spring.

"I shouldn't have barged in on you like that," I apologized as he stood next to me. "You are a much better sport than I am," I added. "I'm not sure how I would have reacted if I woke up and found you watching me."

"I know exactly how you would have reacted." Alexander made a Godzilla-like monster face and we both cracked up knowing he was right.

Alexander moved his chair and place setting next to mine. Jameson entered the room pushing a squeaky-wheeled metal cart carrying a covered sterling silver serving tray. He removed the lid to reveal two sizzling, dripping red steaks.

"I took the liberty of cooking yours medium-well," Jameson said, serving me. "I assumed you didn't like yours as rare as Alexander's."

I glanced over at Alexander's plate. The barely cooked strip steak was almost floating in a pool of blood.

"Mine is perfect," I said with an oversized grin.

"Isn't it a nice surprise that Raven has come to town?" Jameson asked, spooning out steaming-hot buttered peas.

"It's the perfect way to wake up," Alexander said

with a twinkle in his eyes.

"Will there be anything else?"

"I think we are fine," Alexander stated.

I scooted my chair even closer to Alexander's. I couldn't believe that my boyfriend, who had been so far away for so many days, was now by my side. All the pain I'd felt in the last month or so disappeared.

Alexander seemed ravenous as he tore into his bloody steak. I was reminded each time I was in Alexander's company that I was truly dating a vampire. He had just woken up, while I, on the other hand, had been awake for more than twelve hours. Upon awakening, my boyfriend craved blood the way I craved a caramel latte.

There was so much I wanted to ask Alexander I didn't know where to begin. As we continued to cut into our steaks, I pried for the info I'd missed over our time apart.

"Is Valentine here? What have you been doing? When are you planning on coming home?" I babbled.

"Slow down," he said, tapping my hand.

"Tell me about Valentine. Is he okay?"

"Yes, Valentine is fine. He returned to his family."

I paused, waiting to hear more. But Alexander just winked and took a bite of his sweet potato.

"That's it?" I asked.

Where Becky and I would begin retelling a juicy event by "setting the scene," followed by a description of clothing and dialogue, finishing with "overheard gossip" and our biased commentary, Alexander would simply provide one-word answers. How was I supposed to get a nitty-gritty fleshed-out story this way?

"Is Valentine here or in Romania?" I continued to pry.

"Romania, I guess."

"Did you see Jagger?"

"Yes." Alexander went back to cutting into his meat.

"You did? What did he say? Was he threatening? Where did you meet? In Hipsterville's graveyard?"

"I showed up at his apartment at the Coffin Club. I have to admit, he was surprised," Alexander began. "When he lifted the door open, he saw only me standing before him—Valentine was hanging by the elevator. Jagger was primed for an encounter, his fists clenched, his fangs flashing. But when he saw Valentine next to me, a wave of relief overcame him. I'd never seen him like that. Jagger was so happy to have Valentine safe I think all the blood rushed out of him."

"Wow, you really are a hero," I gushed.

"It was obvious Jagger had mixed feelings that I was the one who had returned Valentine to him. He's spent so much time seeking revenge on me for not having a covenant ceremony with Luna he didn't know how to respond. For the first time I can remember, Jagger and I weren't rivals."

"I wish I'd been there to see it," I said.

He clutched my hand.

"After he hugged his brother," Alexander continued, "Jagger extended his hand to me. It was then that I knew a truce was formed—between him and me *and* our families.

Returning Valentine safely was more important than completing any covenant ceremony."

"Do you think you guys will be friends now?"

Alexander shook his head. "Sadly no. We're polar opposites and don't have much in common. But now that things are peaceful between the two of us, it's probably best for him and me not to see each other for a while so we can keep it that way."

Alexander took a drink from his goblet.

"I am really glad you are here," he said quietly.

"I am too!"

We locked eyes. For a moment it was as if we were the only two people in the world. Billions of people were shopping, driving, living, but the only person I was aware of was the gorgeous guy staring back at me.

Alexander leaned over and gently kissed me. I was so lost in his kiss, I didn't realize my sleeve was sitting in my dinner.

"Here, let me," he said, dabbing his napkin in his water glass and brushing off the butter stain.

"Can't take me anywhere," I joked. "So, when will you be returning to Dullsville?" I hinted. "Tomorrow? Next week?"

"I just have one more thing to take care of. It shouldn't take much longer. I promise. Believe me, it's lonely not being around the people you care about most." Alexander gently smiled at me. I felt a twinge of sadness for him. In Romania he had his family. In Dullsville he had me and

Jameson. But here in Hipsterville, he and Jameson were all alone. "How is your family?" he politely asked.

"Billy Boy misses you like crazy. You're like a hero to him."

"When I return to Dullsville, we'll have to take him to a science fair or a screening of the original *Star Wars*."

I laughed. "See? That is why you're so special. You think about doing what *he* likes to do rather than doing something *I'd* like to do—like dragging him to a rave."

Alexander smiled.

"And Becky?" he continued. "Is she still dating Matt?"

"I think she's picking out her wedding dress as we speak. I'm sure she's counting down the days until graduation so she can elope."

Alexander laughed. "And you? Are you anything like Becky?" His gaze was so deliberate, it nearly bore through my soul.

For once *I* was speechless. I was as much of a giddy and googly-eyed girly girl as Becky ever was. But I couldn't confess that I was weak-kneed in an "I'd tattoo your name on my heart if only my parents would let me" way. I had to appear at least remotely sophisticated.

Alexander, however, was waiting for my response.

"Did you hear that there are crop circles popping up in town?" I asked.

Alexander put down his fork. "Where did you learn that?"

"It's all over the news. Do you think it's aliens?"

He paused. "I guess it could be . . ."

"Well, my aunt Libby and I had a major discussion about it. Guess what my theory is."

"Practical jokers?"

"I think it's vampires, signaling the whereabouts of other vampires."

Alexander's eyes widened and he choked on his water.

"Are you okay?"

He nodded his head and covered his mouth with his napkin.

"It makes perfect sense," I continued. "Who else is up at night while most mortals sleep? And who can see the circles better than bats flying over the horizon?" I said.

Alexander gave me a blank look.

But I was undeterred. "The only thing I haven't figured out is what the crop circles mean." I leaned into Alexander intently. "Are they warning other vampires to stay away or inviting them in?"

Alexander quickly broke our gaze.

Jameson burst into the room carrying a dessert tray, ending my investigation.

"Just in time," Alexander said. "We're finished."

Jameson presented us with two perfectly delectable crème brûlées.

"It's like eating at a five-star restaurant!" I complimented him.

Jameson's pale flesh turned pink as he wheeled back our dinner plates.

"There is so much to do while we are here," I said excitedly, digging into my dessert. "You'll have to meet

Aunt Libby. Then there's Hot Gothics. And of course the Coffin Club!"

Alexander gave me a stern look. "Not the Coffin Club."

"Don't worry, I can get in. I have a fake ID."

"That's not what I meant. A club like that is not a place a girl like you should frequent."

"A girl like me?" I laughed in disbelief. "It's a goth club. It was made for me! Ever since I visited it last time, I dreamed that we could return there together. What could possibly happen?"

"A girl in a bar?" he asked, like I had two heads. "Don't you watch the news?"

"I know," I said, rolling my eyes like I was getting scolded by my parents. "It's not the safest place . . . but—"

"Last time you met Jagger. Remember?"

Alexander had a point. I didn't have the greatest track record with my decisions. My curiosity had drawn my boyfriend's nemesis right to him, creating a lot of danger for him and my family.

"All right," I finally admitted. Disappointed, I chiseled away at the burnt sugar topping stuck to the inside of the bowl.

Alexander placed his ghost white hand on my pale one. "We will go, but *together*."

"Can we go tonight?" I asked, perking up.

"How about tomorrow. I wasn't expecting company, remember?"

"Oh, yes, of course." I remembered intruding on him.

Then I furrowed my brow skeptically and challenged him. "You don't have a hot date, do you?"

"Yes. I do, as a matter of fact."

"You do?"

"Yes, and it is almost ending." Alexander glanced at an antique marble clock sitting on the mantel of the unused fireplace. The clock was barely ticking, and the minute hand was broken. I didn't want my evening to end, but I knew of course it had to. He wiped his mouth with his linen napkin and then grabbed my hand.

"I'm so glad you did come," he said adoringly. "You never fail to surprise me."

"You surprise me, too . . ." I took a deep breath, then asked, "Why are you both still here?"

Just then Jameson returned to collect the dishes.

For the time being, Alexander was off the hook. "Allow me, Miss Raven," Jameson said. Alexander and his butler placed the dishes on the top shelf of the cart.

"Jameson will drive you back to your aunt's apartment."

I glanced at the broken clock, still struggling to figure out the correct time.

"Jameson can drop me off at my aunt's drumming class. It's much closer. I believe you may have met my aunt Libby. She works at Happy Homes."

"That beautiful woman is your aunt? I should have known. She is quite charming . . . just like her niece," said Jameson.

"I look forward to meeting her," Alexander said. Then

with a whisper: "Although you'll have to make a few excuses for me not being seen in the daylight."

"Excuses? I wrote the book! I've got one for every occasion."

Like a Victorian gentleman minus the top hat, white gloves, and British accent, Alexander escorted me out the door and down the rock path while Jameson brought the car around.

"Will I see you tomorrow?" I asked my boyfriend as I snuggled in his arms.

"Of course."

"I miss you already."

"I do, too."

Alexander leaned into me and gave me a long, luxurious good-night kiss. He graciously opened the back door of the Mercedes and helped me step in. As we drove off, Alexander stood in the driveway, the mammoth-sized manor house looming behind him like a medieval monster.

Jameson was kind enough to chauffeur me to Hipsterville's Old Town Folk Music Center, but the short five-mile drive from the manor house to the hippie school of music seemed to take longer than the journey from Dullsville to Hipsterville. If I'd pushed the car myself, we'd have made it faster.

Now that Jameson and I had some quality time, I figured I'd make the most of it. I tried to pump the Creepy Man for info on Valentine and Jagger, but he was as evasive as Alexander.

"That was so kind of you and Alexander to reunite Valentine with his family," I began when we drove past Gerald's Gas Station.

"It was the right thing to do," he said sweetly.

"Did you see Jagger?"

I waited on pins, needles, and piercing, bracing for his response.

"No, I didn't. I left that to Alexander."

So much for the facts on *that* conversation.

"I bet Ruby misses you," I said, referring to my former boss who was now dating Jameson.

Jameson's bulgy eyes brightened in the rearview mirror and his pale face flushed bright red with the mention of her name.

"Has she come for a visit?" I pried.

"Oh, no. We are hoping to return to the Mansion shortly."

"Really, then why did you rent the manor house? You could have just stayed in a hotel."

"I don't stay anywhere that already has a house-keeper," Jameson joked.

I felt as if I were playing a game of tennis with my dad. With all my might, I lobbed the ball over the net only to have it returned so hard I didn't have a chance to swing. Frustrated, I always had to take a moment to collect myself. Time for another serve.

"Do you miss Romania?" I asked.

"Oh yes, it's so beautiful there. But I am also quite happy here, in America. I've met some people that I am quite fond of, Miss Raven."

I knew he was politely referring to Ruby and me.

But I wanted more. What were Alexander's and Jameson's plans?

"Do you think you'll marry Ruby?"

"Uh . . ."

"If so, will you live in the manor house? Or in the Mansion?"

"I'm not planning . . ."

"Well, if you did."

"I suppose . . . it would be up to . . . Why all of the questions, Miss Raven?"

We were volleying steadily now, and it was time for me to end the match. I paused, then asked, "I'm just wondering, what are you and Alexander doing here?"

Jameson pulled the car to the curb in front of the Old Town Folk Music Center. I'd swung too hard, hitting the ball over the fence. The match ended, Jameson the obvious winner.

The rain had subsided and the streetlights and lampposts were dripping wet. Jameson climbed out of the Mercedes and kindly held the door open for me, like I was an A-list starlet arriving at a premiere. The only thing missing were the paparazzi. I waved good-bye and was heading for Old Town when I noticed something flashing at the end of the block—the flickering neon red sign of the Coffin Club. As Jameson puttered down the street, I paused. The sounds of banging drums pulsed out of the music center.

It was as if the blinking neon coffins were drawing me to them, like a vulture to a corpse. No one would be the wiser if I just popped my head in for a nonalcoholic bubbly Execution . . . or two.

4

Return to the Coffin Club

I held my breath in wild anticipation of seeing the Coffin Club up close once again, but when I approached the underground club, I was shocked. More than a hundred young goths were anxiously awaiting admittance to the club—twice as long a line as I remembered it being last time. The procession of clubsters, dressed similarly to me (except sporting different-colored streaks, tattoos, piercings, and shoes), wrapped the block like a line at Disney World. I'd be lucky if I gained entrance before summer break was over.

Frustrated, I began walking toward the end of the line. I was about halfway down the block when I noticed a guy with a cape and vinyl pants bent over, adjusting his monster boots. I snuck in the space before him and tried to appear inconspicuous. I avoided any trouble by standing with my back to him and gazed at the stars and then a few birds flying above the roof of the club. When the birds began to hover instead of fly off, I realized I'd spotted a cluster of bats. How wicked—bats at the Coffin Club!

I checked my watch. Aunt Libby's class was going to end in less than an hour, and it appeared that I'd be spending the time waiting in this never-ending line.

I anxiously shifted back and forth. I peered out toward the club's entrance to see if there was an obvious holdup, but there wasn't anything more than a bouncer checking IDs. It was then I noticed a familiar couple standing at the head of the line. I leaned out, holding my place with one foot like a checkers player holds his place with his finger before making his next move. It was Primus and Poison, two clubsters I'd snuck in front of last time I'd visited the club.

Primus and Poison. How could I forget their names when all I'd ever known were names like Billy, Matt, or Becky?

I took a chance and stepped out of line, racing up to the macabre duo. "Primus! Poison! It's me, Raven!"

The pair scrutinized me. It was clear they wanted to recognize me—after all, I did know their names. But I could tell by their gaze that they couldn't place my face.

"I met you a few months ago, here in line," I said, finagling my way into the crowded line beside them.

"Oh yeah," Primus, a Marilyn Manson look-alike, said, finally remembering. "How are you doing?"

Poison looked at me with venom in her eyes.

"I'm great!" I said to Primus. "It's so cool to see you

again." Then I turned to Poison. "I love your corset! It's beautiful!"

Poison's disposition changed. "I just threw this together."

"No way! You should be a model for *Gothic Beauty*."

One could hear the sudden sound of a motorcycle's engine revving above the other street noises and the throbbing music bleeding out of the Coffin Club. A Harley-Davidson Night Rod shot up the street and screeched to a halt in an empty VIP space right in front of the club. The hot rod had a sleek and sexy design, black-walled tires with orange pinstripes. The rider took off his helmet, emblazoned with a white skull and crossbones, unleashing shoulder-length jagged purple hair with black undertones. Wearing dark Ray-Bans and dressed in stud-and-chain-riddled leather pants and jacket, the motorcycle rider confidently hopped off his Night Rod, nodded to the bouncer, and walked right into the club as if he owned it.

"Who's he?" I wondered aloud. "A celeb? I didn't recognize him."

"They all think they are movie stars here now," Primus said.

"Yes, this club has tripled in size in the last few months. And so has the attitude," Poison added.

The line inched forward, and before I knew it we were presenting the burly bouncer with our IDs.

The gatekeeper immediately stamped the image of a bat on Primus's and Poison's hands and strapped barbed-wire-shaped bracelets on their wrists, but he scrutinized my card like he was checking a passport at an international airport.

Poison doubled back and got right in the bouncer's face. "She comes here all the time," she said. "I can't believe you don't remember her."

The bouncer lifted his gaze back to me, his expression one of disdain, then shifted it to the waiting line, sporting streaks in various colors of the gothic rainbow.

"I had blue hair last time," I said.

"Oh, that was you?" he asked seriously.

He stamped my hand with the Coffin Club bat and wrapped a band around my wrist. I had gained passage to the Coffin Club. We slipped behind the bouncer, headed past the bloodred carpet and rope and two skeleton greeters, and before I knew it I was walking through the black wooden coffin-shaped doors.

"Thanks," I said to Poison. "Everyone says I look younger than I am. I bet you get that a lot, since you have such flawless skin."

Poison's ghost white face lit up. She put her arm around me. "I'll buy the first round," she said.

The Coffin Club was still morbidly magical. Neon headstones flashed against black spray-painted cement walls. Pale mannequins, dressed in antique clothing or Victorian suits or bound in leather, hung from the rafters. Music pulsed hard throughout the club as if the DJ were trying to wake the dead. A balcony, the place where I'd first encountered Alexander's nemesis, Jagger, loomed over the vampire-wannabe crowded dance floor, blood-filled amulets swinging from necks like Olympic medals.

But Primus was right. The Coffin Club had changed in the last few months. The club was packed, black wall to black wall, with clubsters. The thick dry ice permeated the air like a Jack the Ripper London fog, making it difficult to see. And where, as last time, I got stares as I ventured through the club, this time the clubsters were intensely partying and seemingly uninterested in a newbie.

I followed Primus and Poison to the bar, but other eager patrons pushed their way in front of me, leaving me to fall behind. I could see their heads above the crowd as I squeezed between the clubsters. When I thought I'd finally reached them, I realized I'd been following another couple the entire time. I popped out at the mini–flea market, where for a small price a clubster could buy anything from an amulet to a sit-down with a numerologist. The packed dance floor was next to the row of sellers, but the bar was nowhere in sight.

I squeezed my way back between the dancing and drinking clubsters, past the giant tombstone-shaped restroom doors marked MONSTERS and GHOULS. I finally saw a wall filled with bottles, spiderwebs clinging to them. I knew I had found the holy grail. But the bar was so jammed with thirsty customers it was impossible to see who was bartending or where Primus and Poison were located. I squished my way through. Just as a girl was sliding off a tombstone-shaped barstool, I jumped on it.

A guy sitting next to me spun around. He was wearing more eyeliner than Alice Cooper, and it didn't look as good on him as it did on the elder rocker.

"I'll buy you whatever you want," he said, slurring his way into my face and space.

I spotted the bartender, Romeo, but neither my barmate nor I attracted his attention.

Romeo responded to every wave of a ten-dollar bill but continued to ignore us. When he passed by for the hundredth time, I leaned over the bar and grabbed his tattooed arm.

Since Alexander and Jameson had been mum about all things Maxwell, I thought this was my chance to get some inside scoop. "Did Jagger go back to Romania?" I asked.

Romeo, holding a beer in each hand, glared at me. The mention of Jagger's name gave him pause. Like Primus and Poison, he didn't recognize me.

"Who wants to know?" he asked suspiciously.

"Raven. Is he in town? Or did he go back to Romania?"

"Raven . . . Your name sounds familiar."

I realized I shouldn't have let Romeo know I was looking for Jagger. I wasn't a regular clubster; I was the girlfriend of Jagger's nemesis. Alexander had already reunited Valentine with him. Now it appeared as if I was stirring up trouble. How could I have been so stupid?

"I'll have a Medieval Massacre, and the lady will have—," my barmate began.

"I'll be right back," I said, knowing I wouldn't return.

It was time to call it a night. I'd lost Primus and Poison. I'd been asking about locations of nefarious vampires. And I was an underage girl alone at a bar. I'd better arrive at Old Town before this black-fingernailed Cinderella turned into a pumpkin.

Fatigue set in as I headed for the entrance doors. It was starting to hit me that when I'd woken up this morning, I was in Dullsville. I began to feel dizzy as I pushed and squeezed my way through the fog-filled club, my safety pins getting tangled on other clubsters' chains. When I glanced up, I'd reached a wall that was unfamiliar but had a coffin-shaped door. I tried to open it, but it was stuck. I turned the knob and pushed my body against it.

The door flung open and I stumbled into a barely lit area. It took me several steps before I realized that instead of exiting into the street, I had entered a dimly lit corridor.

I would have turned back, but I heard music (different from the song being played in the Coffin Club) pulsing from the other end. Perhaps it was coming from Jagger's apartment—the very one he had shown me when I visited the club on my last trip. It would take only a moment for me to find out. A single overhead naked bulb lit the cryptic corridor, and graffiti lined the cement walls like an urban overpass. When I reached the end of the corridor, I discovered another smaller tunnellike path, with arched stone walls and a very narrow, steep staircase that plummeted into darkness. I let the rusty handrail go untouched and crept down the stairs. They led to a single wooden dungeon door. Written in bloodred spray-painted letters was: DEAD END.

Was this someone's office? Or perhaps another entrance to the apartment Jagger had been living in?

I pressed my ear to the coffin-lid door. I could hear a mixture of music and voices.

I slowly turned the knob and pushed the door, but it wouldn't budge. I heard some voices behind me and the sound of footsteps descending the stairs. It was a dead end—I had nowhere to go. I knew at any moment I might be kicked out of the club and perhaps Hipsterville altogether—if I lived to tell.

Two guys with the complexion of corpses, one blond, one redhead, confronted me. "Can't get in?" the blond one asked.

"I forgot my key," I said flippantly.

"It's okay, I have mine."

He unclipped a skeleton key swinging from a chain attached to his studded belt.

"Getting in is easy," the blond said.

"That is, if you make it past Dragon," his friend retorted.

"But getting out is harder," the blond warned.

I didn't know what lay on the other side or why a key was required to unlock the door. I'd also never heard of a guard shielding the inside of a door.

The coffin lid creaked open. We stepped into a dark and dingy foyer where we were greeted by a monstrous-looking bouncer the size of a small dinosaur. Black fabric hung behind him like at a car wash, blocking any view of what he was guarding.

The bouncer's head was shaved, and inked on it was the head of a dragon, its reptilian wings breaking out of his white tank top and wrapping his Terminator biceps. I didn't dare ask to see the bottom half of the fiery dragon.

The two corpselike guys showed him their keys, walked through a slit in the fabric, then disappeared.

"Where is yours?" he grumbled.

"He has it," I said, pointing to the guy I'd followed in. "Please, they're waiting for me."

He paused, inspecting me to see if I was worthy of passing. I'd flashed him my best "Don't make me ask to see the manager" face when the door opened again and a group of clubsters, draped in black and sporting white fangs, entered.

"Next time, keep it on you," he said. "Otherwise you'll be banned."

I pushed through the fabric before Dragon changed his mind. What lay on the other side blew my mind—it was a massive underground tomb. An ancient-looking subterranean cemetery, with serpentine catacombs and graves dug out in the stone walls and dirt floors, like something unearthed on the History Channel. It was creepy, dark and dangerous. In the center, a sunken dance floor with a hard-rocking band played on a fluorescent-lit stage. Spray-painted in red on the wall behind the bandmates were the words THE DUNGEON with a pair of real shackles and chains hanging down. Suspended above was a candelabra chandelier where a disco ball might be. Surrounding the dance floor were hallowed tombs carved into the walls, like a skeletal morgue, and fifteen-foot-high stone archways leading to cavelike rooms. Where mummies would have been buried instead were live bodies, drinking, smoking, and making out. Each cave was lined with black or red velvet and had puffy leather couches with canoodling couples. More than a few entranceways spawned darkened tunnels, their destinations unknown from my vantage point. Some bore signs—THE EXECUTIONER'S LOUNGE, THE TORTURE CHAMBER, DRACULA'S DEN—while others remained bare like an unmarked grave.

As morbid as the buried club was, the clubsters themselves were stylishly ghoulish. The dancers were uniformly pale, blue lips covered with red gloss. The clubsters ranged in dress from goth to punk to gothic Lolitas. Each appeared to be more seductive than the next. The club's stone walls dripped with danger, while its inhabitants oozed with sensuality. Though its existence and location were secretive and secluded, I'd stumbled upon a cryptically wicked party scene. This club was far more intimate and sinister than its sister club above.

And unlike the patrons upstairs, these ghost white clubsters appeared inviting. Guys and girls alike checked me out as I made my way through. Some stared at me as if they guessed I didn't have a key to enter, while other oglers didn't seem to care.

Guys were kissing girls' necks, wrists, and every place with a prominent vein as the girls smiled back with delight.

This crowd was definitely a whole lot friendlier. "Hi. Want to dance?" A guy approached me as I was avoiding stepping into a grave, while another girl, her nose as long as a witch's, just followed me. "I haven't seen you around before. Are you single? I know the perfect guy for you."

But instead of obliging them, I snuck up to the bar and hopped on a barstool.

A bartender, his hair flowing down to the dirt floor, set a black Dungeon bar napkin in front of me. "We have imports or domestic."

"Uh . . . how about local?"

The bartender laughed. "It's ladies' night. Girls drink free."

I was as thirsty as a bloodless vampire.

"In that case . . . something nonalcoholic."

"Sure . . . why dilute it."

He grabbed a vintage green bottle, poured its contents into a pewter glass, then pushed the drink to me.

The drink smelled peculiar. I was hoping it would taste like supersweet Kool-Aid, but it appeared to have the consistency of tomato juice.

I touched it with my finger and examined it closely.

Then I realized it was neither Kool-Aid nor tomato juice—it was blood.

Was this a mistake, or perhaps a practical joke?

"Can I get some water, too?" I asked, flagging him down.

"Don't you like it?"

"It's delicious," I said, not wanting to draw attention to myself. "I'd like to finish it off with a glass of water."

He placed another goblet next to my blood-filled one while I rubbed my hand with a bacterial wipe underneath the bar.

I smelled the new glass. Who knows—it could have been filled with whiskey. There wasn't any noticeable scent, so I took a small sip. I was in luck. It was ordinary Hipsterville tap water. I guzzled it down, then placed a tip on the bar. I was getting ready to hop off the stool when someone put their hand on my shoulder.

A slender guy with a five o'clock shadow sat at the bar next to me. "Where are you from?"

I rolled my eyes and recoiled my shoulder from his hand.

"I don't mean that as a pickup line; I really meant it—where are you from?"

"Are you taking a survey?"

"As a matter of fact . . ."

I didn't feel like telling a stranger my personal address. It was enough that Jagger had followed me home from the Coffin Club last time I'd visited Hipsterville. I didn't want Five O'clock Shadow showing up at my house, shaved or not.

"You'll have to find someone else for your survey."

"I've never seen you here before. How did you find out about this place?"

"A little bat told me."

He cracked a smile.

"And you?" I asked, only to be polite.

"The crop circles. Then I knew there was a population of our kind here."

"Aliens?" I asked.

The stranger laughed again. I was intrigued by his

response, but I knew if I pressed him for more info, he'd interpret our continuing conversation as a come-on.

"Let me buy you a drink," he said, moving close.

"Thanks anyway; I'm not staying."

"You're cautious. I understand . . . We all are. That's why the Coffin Club is the hottest underground club. We can all be ourselves. By the way, my name is Leopold."

"Uh . . . I'm . . ."

I felt something vibrating in my purse. I reached in—it was my cell. Saved by the bell—or in this case vibration. "I have to take this," I said, leaving the bar. I flipped my cell open and snuck under a stone archway.

"Raven?" It was Aunt Libby. I could barely hear her. "How are you?"

"Hi, Aunt Libby," I shouted back. "I'm fine."

"What are you doing? I can hardly hear you."

I sauntered through the catacombs, heading away from the noisy dance floor.

"I have your stereo cranked."

"You'll have to turn it down. I don't want my neighbors to complain."

"Of course. I'll turn it off as soon as we hang up."

"Are you having a good time?"

"Can you talk louder?" I asked, holding my other ear closed with my index finger.

"Are you having fun? I'm sure you're bored to tears."

"It's not too bad," I bellowed back, continuing to walk.

"I wish you had come to class with me. Our teacher was from Kenya. He was truly amazing."

"Don't worry about me. I'm having a great time by myself," I said truthfully.

"What? I can't hear you."

"I'm having a great time," I shouted as a few clubsters dressed in cosplay outfits passed me.

"Class will be letting out shortly. I'll see you soon."

"Take your time, Aunt Libby."

"What?"

"You don't have to rush on account of me."

"I can't hear you. We'll talk when I get home. See you soon." She hung up before I had a chance to stall her departure.

It was imperative that I beat Aunt Libby home.

I dropped my cell in my purse and realized I'd lost my sense of direction. Was the Dungeon dance floor to the right or the left? I had a fifty-fifty chance of making the correct choice. Naked bulbs lit the way through the stone tunnel, and a few more catacombs splintered off. I'd been so focused on my conversation with Aunt Libby that I hadn't made any mental directional notes. I needed a trail of bread crumbs.

I noticed some skulls lining the tunnel like a kitchen border. I didn't remember seeing them when I was talking on the phone, but then again, I wasn't looking.

The tunnel was dimly lit and confining. The stone walls leaned as if caving in on me as I paced in indecision.

I heard some voices and laughter coming from one end, so I followed them. Cautiously I crept through the catacombs, trying not to trip on the uneven terrain. The winding tunnel dumped into a small room. THE COVE. A dozen or so clubsters, their backs to me, were listening to what I thought might have been a stand-up comic. I was curious why they chose to listen instead of jamming on the dance floor.

But this was no ordinary blue-jean-wearing comedian. He wore a dark hoodie, pulled over his head, obscuring his deathly pale face, and he wasn't making the crowd laugh.

"The Dungeon should take a new direction. Why hide in obscurity when there is so much more we can do?" he challenged. Catching the glare of a single stagelight was a gold skeleton key dangling from a black lanyard around his neck like a backstage pass to a rock concert.

"I agree. Why deny who we are?" a girl asked, a snake wrapped around her neck like a mink stole.

"That's why this club is so important, so we can be ourselves," another began.

"But the Dungeon is a secret and safe place we can call our own."

"Isn't it time we make ourselves known?" the snake whisperer argued, caressing the reptile. "Many of us are becoming frustrated remaining hidden."

"But many others feel safer among ourselves," one clubster admitted.

"We don't get along with outsiders," another said.

"Maybe it's time that we try," a girl in the front row said.

"So we can be like them and lose our identity?" another asked.

The tension grew from both sides. The speaker held his hands up. "Calm down. We must all be united."

A guy hanging next to me asked, "What do you think?"

All at once the group was staring straight at me. The snake, still coiled around his owner, hissed.

"I think it's time for me to get back to the dance floor!"

I stole my way back into the once deadly tunnel. My eyes didn't have a chance to adjust to the darkness and I bumped into a pair of girls. I stiffened but was too tired for a barroom brawl.

"Excuse me," I said. "Do you know the way back to the dance floor?"

The girls, unlike the Pradabees at Dullsville High, weren't confrontational. Instead I felt a warmth and friendliness emanating from them.

The two girls appeared to be my age. One wore an indigo blue corset dress, while the other sported a baby doll dress and thigh-high silver-laced boots. Their purple-hued vampy makeup dramatically accentuated their Draculine features. One had long red curly hair and the other's jet black hair was straight as a blade.

"Follow me," the girl in the corset dress directed, linking our arms. "I'm Onyx, and this is Scarlet. What's your name?" She flashed a gorgeous smile, revealing a tiny black onyx jewel embedded on one of her fangs.

"Wow—where did you get those?" I began. "They look so real."

She flashed her fangs again. "It is. We can totally get yours done, too."

I was taken aback. Onyx was referring to the jewel, while I was referring to her fangs.

"How do you find your way around the club?" I asked.

"It took us an eternity," Scarlet replied.

Before I knew it, I'd made it safely to the center of the club, two new friends in tow.

"Thank you so much," I said. "Now I'll be on my way—"

Their bright expressions turned sallow. "Don't you want to dance?"

Here I was hanging out with two of the coolest girls I'd ever met—when I'd been excluded by cliques my whole life. It was thrilling to be immediately accepted as myself. And I didn't know when I'd get a chance to come to the Dungeon again.

"Okay, one song!" I relented.

We thrashed around and giggled like we'd been best friends since childhood. I envisioned what life would have been like for me if Scarlet and Onyx had grown up in Dullsville. We'd have sleepovers during the day, paint our nails by moonlight, and gossip in the graveyard.

We rocked so hard, I thought my fake tattoos were going to fall off. The vampire theme was taken to the extreme in the Dungeon. Clubsters writhed together as if drinking in each other's souls. As lustful guys' lips lay on giddy girls' necks, it was unclear where one clubster began and the other ended.

I was intoxicated by the music, the dangerous feel of the club, and my acceptance by Scarlet and Onyx. Then I noticed the time. "I really have to go."

"Already? But we can dance until dawn," Scarlet offered, tossing her luscious thick red curly hair off her shoulder.

"I can't. I'm supposed to meet someone."

"Is he dreamy?" Onyx asked.

"Is he like us?" Scarlet prodded.

I was too embarrassed to say I was meeting my aunt.

"I'll give you my number." Scarlet opened my purse, pulled out my cell, and punched in a ten-digit number. "Call whenever you want, except during the day. My parents despise being woken up."

She hugged me hard, as did Onyx.

I hated to leave. Besides being with Alexander, I was having the best time of my life. I was reluctant to leave my discovery of the Dungeon behind.

When I stepped off the dance floor I noticed my boot had come unlaced. I hobbled off to one side, avoiding any clubsters who might trip over my long shoestrings. I had kicked up my boot on a chair and leaned on the archway for support when I sensed someone's piercing gaze. Buried in the shadows of a small cavelike lounge, I could barely see the silhouette of a person sitting alone. Curious, I inched forward. From a safe distance, I peered through the darkness. A candelabra perched on the table gently illuminated the figure. First I saw motorcycle boots, crossed at the ankle, resting on the dirt floor, then tight black leather pants, like cellophane. I could see the sleeves of his motorcycle jacket, his chain, and his studded arms folded. I stepped a tiny bit closer and leaned into the ray of light. Purple hair flopped over black sunglasses. He seemed to be staring straight at me. It took a moment, but I broke his binding gaze and retreated into the safety of the shadows, or so I hoped.

Why was the motorcycle guy checking me out? And sitting alone like he was waiting to hold court?

I felt strangely drawn to him. His stare was magnetic.

Several rough-looking clubsters approached him—but instead of greeting him like one of the guys by slapping him on the arm or high-fiving him, they all nodded and entered the small chamber, sat down at the table around him, and waited for him to speak.

I desperately wanted to hear their secret conversation and get a handle on who or what this biker was all about.

"He doesn't have any idea about what vampires truly need," one clubster told the biker.

"I think it's time we do something," another said.

"Before he ruins our plans," a third added.

The purple-haired biker leaned in, out of earshot.

The cagey guys were listening to him so intently, I could tell they were as entranced as I was. If the biker was these barbaric clubsters' leader, I could only imagine that I'd encountered someone twice as dangerous as Jagger and Valentine.

I felt my heart race again throughout my body when I realized my cell phone was vibrating. Aunt Libby again.

Everyone, except for the biker, turned and glared at me. But the rock star biker dude remained still. It was as if he knew I had been standing there the whole time.

I quickly headed for the archway leading back to the dance floor when all at once someone was standing in front of me, blocking my way.

I took a breath and looked up. His purple hair flopped down, seductively, over his Ray-Bans. His stern, hypnotic gaze bore through the dark lenses. There was something powerful about the mysterious stranger. He smelled like Obsession and towered over me in his thick motorcycle boots.

"How did you get in?" he asked in a heavy Romanian accent.

"Do you own the club?"

"No, but I might." His leather jacket crackled as he folded his arms. "I haven't seen you before." His head lowered and it appeared he was checking out my neck. "I suspect you don't belong."

I fiddled with my earring, covering my smooth, bite-free neck with my palm. I felt slightly intimidated by him, but it didn't prevent me from talking back.

"How would you know?" I challenged.

His glasses and hair cast a shadow over his face, making him hard to read. I wasn't sure if he broke a smile. By his body language, I knew he was serious. "It is best that you leave. Membership to our club comes at a very high price. But perhaps I can explain more over a drink."

"No thanks. I already have a boyfriend."

"Then he is a very lucky guy," he complimented me. "My name is Phoenix Slater," he said, extending his hand and grabbing mine. "And you are?"

"Leaving," I said, pulling my hand away.

I had made it halfway to the Dungeon door when he slithered his arm around me. Angry, I spun around but wasn't prepared for who I now confronted. Staring back at me were one metallic green eye and one ice blue eye. Jagger Maxwell.

I gasped. It had been a few months since I'd seen Alexander's nemesis up close and personal.

Jagger looked exactly the same—white hair with red tips, as if they'd been dipped in blood. Three silver rings pierced his left ear, and a tattoo on his arm read POSSESS. He was holding the dark hoodie.

He closed in on me like a spider to a fly.

"What are you doing here?" I asked, moving back.

"What are *you* doing here?" he demanded, slithering close.

"I thought you were in Romania."

"I thought you were in Alexander's arms."

"I came here to see—"

"Yes?" He watched my lips intensely, waiting for my response.

"My aunt."

"Does your aunt belong to this club?" he asked, mocking me. "What is she, forty? Fifty? I don't see anyone dancing with a walker."

"She's not here, doofus," I said. "She lives in town, but you'd better—"

"I have no interest in your aunt. You, however . . ." He inhaled deeply, as if he were breathing me in, then licked his deadly pale lips. "I'm curious why you are here. This club is for members only. But once you join, membership lasts for an eternity. Unless . . ."

"Unless what?"

"Unless you've already joined."

Before I had a chance to stop him, he placed his cold hands against my chin and turned my head from one side to the other, inspecting my neck.

"Let go!"

"I didn't think so. You really shouldn't be here. This is not a place for your kind."

"I don't have a kind."

"Too bad. Isn't this what you've always dreamed of?" He stared into my eyes and traced the neckline of my dress with his black-tipped fingernail. He licked his lips and flashed his fangs.

Phoenix pushed between us. He and Jagger locked eyes before Jagger backed away.

Dozens of clubsters gathered around, half on Jagger's side, the others flanking Phoenix, as if awaiting a deadly fight.

I didn't know which side to choose. Even though I knew Jagger was nefarious, I at least had an idea of who I was dealing with. But as the tension grew between the two, I knew it was best to leave.

I escaped and hid behind the black curtain a few yards away. When I caught my breath, I peered inside the slit in the fabric.

I wasn't quite sure what kind of club I'd stumbled into, but I had an idea. Blood-filled drinks, flashing fangs, a club where membership lasts an eternity. There was only one way to be sure.

I reached into my purse and pulled out Ruby's compact. I angled it behind me. I took a deep breath and peered into the reflected glass. I froze. The crowded club and dance floor were empty.

I'd just entered the *real* Coffin Club.

5

The Catacombs

After I whisked past Dragon, who was screening members, I sprinted up the steep staircase and out the Coffin Club's main entrance. I heard the sound of a motorcycle engine behind me as I tore down the street to find Aunt Libby outside the Old Town Folk Music Center, holding a large African drum under her arm, very surprised to see me.

I crashed on Aunt Libby's futon, but sleep did not immediately overtake me. In the middle of the night, I heard a motorcycle charging down the street. I sat up and peered out the pale blue curtained window. There were no signs of Phoenix or any other Harley rider. I fell back on the mattress but was still tightly wound by the night's events swirling around in my mind.

71

Just when I thought I'd seen everything, or knew all there was for a mortal to know about the Underworld, I had stumbled into another unearthly adventure. I thought my life had become rich enough when I found out Alexander's vampire identity. Then I encountered Jagger, Luna, and Valentine and their bloodthirsty ways. Who ever would have thought, living and growing up in Dullsville (where the biggest event was the annual spring carnival), that one day, not only would these events happen to me, but I would encounter a club where vampires were accepting me as one of their own.

It had been one thing to hang out with Luna and encounter Jagger in Dullsville. Tonight was like nothing else I'd experienced. Instead of going to the mall with Becky, I'd been dancing with vampires. Immersed in their world versus meeting a few in mine, I got to see what the Underworld was like. Without the threat of mortals, they were free to be themselves. Flirting, drinking, and partying like any other clubster in an alternative club, except one thing—the clientele were immortal bloodsucking vampires.

I replayed the night's events in my mind. I wondered why Jagger had remained in Hipsterville. Wasn't his time better spent back in Romania with Luna and Valentine? And who was this Phoenix character? Why was I, along with a rough gang of vampires, so drawn to him? Was he more trouble than Jagger? And what was his gang asking him to do?

The worst thing about my new discoveries was that I wouldn't be able to tell Alexander anything. Not about

Primus and Poison or my visit to the Coffin Club. And mostly, I wouldn't be able to utter a word about my entrance into the Dungeon, meeting Onyx and Scarlet, or my encounter with Jagger and Phoenix.

This dark and deadly Underworld was exactly why Alexander left Romania in the first place. He was an outsider in the carnivorous world he'd been born into. If he knew that right under his nose there was a private club of vampires, he might feel lonelier.

Perhaps Alexander already knew about the crop circles and the underground club. Maybe that was the reason he and Jameson were staying in Hipsterville—to see if anything would happen. But then why would he have been so secretive and not told me?

Maybe it was I who should come clean. Tell him everything—from Jagger to Phoenix. But then I would risk Alexander becoming involved with the Dungeon, further delaying his return to Dullsville. For now, it was best to leave things as they were.

The plastic bracelet on my arm would be a dead giveaway to Alexander about my sneak-in to the club. I hated to keep a secret from him, but I had to think things through before I made the right decision.

If I cut the bracelet off, I didn't stand a chance of being let back in. I got up and grabbed my suitcase and snatched out a small Black Catz travel bag. Inside was a Hello Batty terry cloth wristband. I slid it on and buried the plastic bracelet safely underneath.

I imagined myself back at the manor house, Alexander

holding me in his arms as we lay hidden away in his coffin in his monster-sized attic room. Nothing from the outside world or the Underworld could distract us from the love that we shared together.

I wasn't even sure what time it was; I only knew I was back at the Dungeon. The catacombs were filled with vampires—lurking, thirsting, hungering, stalking—hidden behind archways and in full view. Suddenly I was surrounded by a gang of vampire clubsters. The dance floor was converted into a medieval baptism of sorts. A covered coffin was lying in the center of the dirt dance floor enclosed by six-foot-high candelabras. At the helm, two hooded members were holding court in ornate hand-carved thrones fit for vampire kings. Clubsters began chanting, "New blood, new blood."

"What's going on?" I asked. I finally found Onyx and Scarlet in the crowd of chanting vampires.

"We're initiating a new member," Onyx revealed excitedly.

My stomach caved in. I wasn't ready to bear witness to

someone going under "the fang."

"Who?" I asked.

Scarlet laughed. "It's you!"

The crowd turned to me and all of a sudden clubsters were lifting me up and passing me over them like I was Queen of the Mosh Pit.

The clubsters continued to chant, "New blood, new blood."

I did my best to fight off the sea of black and blood-red-fingernailed hands, but two fists and two combat-booted feet didn't stand a chance against the force of a crowd of hungry vampires.

"I'm not ready!" I cried. "I'm waiting for Alexander!"

Before I knew it, they lowered me onto the coffin and held my arms at bay, red-eyed vampires chanting, "New blood, new blood" around me.

"Get off!" I cried, but the clubsters held my arms and legs tightly. I noticed two familiar faces in the crowd around me—Primus and Poison.

"Primus! Poison!" I called to them. "Tell them I'm not ready to join!"

"We told you the Coffin Club had changed," Primus said.

"You should have stayed with us, but instead you got curious and opened the Dungeon door," Poison said. "Now we are members, too!" She flashed her fangs at me.

A pair of cloaked members arose from their thrones

and approached me. The smaller one held a goblet with one hand and with his other dipped his fingers into the cup. Then, like dripping wax, he drizzled the warm liquid on my neck, making soft strokes, marking me with a bloody **X**.

"No," I cried. "Get off of me!"

The vampire took off his hood. All I saw was white hair and two red eyes. It was Jagger.

I turned away. There in the crowd staring straight back at me was Alexander. I sensed his disappointment in finding me here in the Coffin Club. I reached out, but he backed away and disappeared into the crowd.

The other hooded member approached me. A gold-fanged female unveiled his hood and jagged purple hair flopped out.

Phoenix grinned a menacing grin, his fangs as sharp as knives. He leaned into me and plunged his teeth into my neck.

"No!" I tried to cry, but I was voiceless.

I awoke with a gasp, in a pool of perspiration, my hands around my neck.

Multicolored Grateful Dead bear figures danced on the fireplace mantel. An African drum lay next to an antique rocker. Light from the window shone through as the sun began rising over the trees. I was out of breath, but I sighed with relief. I was locked away safe in my aunt's apartment, lying on the futon in her living room, underneath the sun's blanket of protection. I yanked the comforter over my head and tried desperately to fall asleep and dream of the only vampire I trusted, Alexander Sterling.

That afternoon I was hanging out in a pair of sweats at Aunt Libby's breakfast table and nursing a cup of coffee when I heard the jostling of keys outside my aunt's door.

Aunt Libby entered with her Happy Homes blazer and a few bags of groceries.

"I'd ask you what you want to do today," she said as I helped her bring them to the kitchen, "but the day is almost over. So how about tonight?"

"Well . . ."

"I'm sure you're still tired from yesterday, so if you want to stay in . . ."

When Alexander and I were in the manor house having dinner the night before, he'd promised me that he'd take me to the Coffin Club tonight. I didn't want to ditch Aunt Libby, and though I was still freaked out about my nightmare of the vampire-filled Dungeon, I was still dying to see Alexander and fulfill my dream of dancing together at the Coffin Club.

However, my aunt was holding out for my response, and "I already have plans" was not what she was waiting to hear. Here I was, staying at her house, eating her food, and I'd become so selfish that I was making plans without her.

"Whatever you want to do," I finally said. "The night is yours."

But instead of answering, Aunt Libby continued to unload the groceries.

"We can see a movie," I suggested. "Go to a jazz club. Visit some boutiques."

Still, my aunt wasn't as excited as I'd thought she'd be at my ideas.

"Or if you have something else . . ."

"I do have something else," she said anxiously.

"Then we can do that."

"It's a date."

"A date? With Devon?"

She nodded. "I'm a terrible aunt," she said. "Devon called me at lunch today. He asked me out for tonight and before I knew it I had said yes."

"That's okay."

"No, it was the wrong thing to do. I'll call and cancel," she said, reaching for her cordless phone on the kitchen counter.

"Don't even think about it," I said, seizing it first.

"Then you'll have to come."

"Are you kidding? On your first date? Even I know that would be a disaster."

"Please, I can't leave you behind again. A sixteen-year-old doesn't want to hang out at her aunt's apartment alone. I know that's why you snuck out last night and showed up at my class—because you were bored."

A sixteen-year-old also doesn't want to go on a date with her aunt and her new beau, either, I thought but couldn't say. "I won't be bored tonight. I promise. I have summer reading I can get a head start on."

She raised her eyebrow. "You are getting to be more like your father than I thought you were."

"Or at least Billy Boy."

Alexander and I arrived at the Coffin Club to find Phoenix's motorcycle already parked in the VIP spot. "Wow, that's a cool bike," Alexander commented when we passed it. "What do you think?"

"I think it's cool, but not half as cool as you are," I replied, squeezing his hand as we continued to walk by the procession of clubgoers.

I imagined Phoenix waltzing into the club as if he were royalty while my boyfriend and I stood at the back of the line.

But really, where else on earth would I rather be? Alexander was by my side, and soon I would have my wish come true. It would be a night to remember.

Still, I couldn't help but let my mind stray. Alexander, after all, was a vampire. He could get a key and lifetime membership to the Dungeon in two shakes of a fang.

However, if I told Alexander I'd already been there, without him, he'd be furious. And he would know I'd been to the underground club if I mentioned seeing Jagger. As far as Alexander knew, Jagger had returned to Romania, and likewise Jagger probably thought Alexander was back in Dullsville. It wasn't my place to disclose their locations. I'd caused Alexander enough problems in the past—I had led Jagger from Hipsterville right to Alexander. It would be difficult, but I'd have to keep my black lips sewn shut.

Alexander and I proudly entered the Coffin Club, hand in hand, like we were stars entering a party. We were so used to being outsiders, it felt good to finally enter a place filled with people who looked just like us.

I felt euphoric standing underneath the lifeless mannequins with my very own vampire boyfriend. The crowd and music were even more pumped up than they were the previous night. This time the clubsters weren't so focused on themselves. In fact, the girls were ogling my date! At first I thought it was fun, as if I'd arrived on the arm of a rock star. After a few minutes of every cleavage-showing, miniskirt-wearing girl checking him out, I was getting jealous. Didn't they know I was standing right next to him? A few guys looked me over, but every girl we passed stared at Alexander like he was Criss Angel performing magic.

Finally I drew him over to the bar. "Don't you notice that?"

"Notice what?" he asked naively.

"The girls?"

"What girls?"

"Hello! You were worried about bringing me to a bar when all along I should have been concerned about bringing you."

"I don't know what you are talking about," he said seriously.

"The girls are drooling all over you!"

Alexander blushed, then laughed gently.

"Well, there is only one girl I want to be with and she's right here," he said.

The bartender, a robust woman who appeared to have been bartending since they invented beer, asked us for our drink order.

Alexander and I cooled off with nonalcoholic Guillotines.

Alexander looked heavenly against the backdrop of neon tombstones, his soulful eyes gently gazing into mine. He appeared as happy as I'd ever seen him, as if he didn't want to be anywhere else in the world but together at this club. His arm lay protectively around me, our fingers entwined. Yet I felt a pang of loneliness for Alexander. He spent so much time up in his attic room, alone, whether in Dullsville or Hipsterville, his only full-time companion being his creepy yet caring butler. I was excited to be part of Alexander's night life tonight.

Of course, I couldn't help but wonder what was going on down in the Dungeon. Were new members being brought in? Where were they from? Were Phoenix and Jagger getting in each other's faces? I was dying to share the underground club with Alexander, but a culture full of bloodthirsty vampires is exactly what Alexander had left behind in Romania. He was much happier in an environment where mortals dressed like vampires rather than one where vampires dressed like mortals. And even if I'd wanted to, I wasn't sure I'd be able to find the secret coffin-shaped door.

"You seem distracted," Alexander remarked.

"I was just thinking of you, actually."

"Well, you don't have to think about me. I'm right here." He leaned over and gave me a lip-lock that sent shivers down to my boots.

He placed our drinks on the bar, grabbed my hand, and led me to the dance floor.

For the next hour, we danced, thrashed, and jammed, all the while forgetting the difference between mortal and immortal.

As the DJ spun the end of one song into the start of another, I took a moment to catch my breath. Stretching out my neck, I spotted a figure up on the balcony, seated on a coffin-shaped couch, the candelabra before him illuminating his ghost white hair, the ends bloodred.

I grabbed Alexander by the arm and dragged him to another end of the dance floor, hidden from the balcony's view. I didn't want Jagger to spill the beans to Alexander that I'd been spotted at the Dungeon. I wanted to tell Alexander on my own.

"What did you do that for?"

"I just thought it would be fun if we got cozy."

"But it's so crowded back here, it's hard to breathe.

Why don't we go over there and relax," he suggested, pointing to couches on the side of the dance floor.

"That's all right . . ."

"You look a bit tired. It's okay if we take a break." He pulled me out from underneath the balcony's overhang.

Alexander was heading for the main part of the dance floor, in full view of the balcony.

"No," I said, tugging him back.

"What's wrong?"

"I want to sit down."

"But the seats are over there."

Alexander looked at me with curious and confused eyes. If I told him that Jagger was still in town, he'd stay in Hipsterville even longer. I'd be forcing him to remain in town indefinitely, perhaps longer than whatever was mysteriously holding him here in the first place.

"C'mon," he said. "Let's go."

But I was more concerned about Alexander's safety. Even though he and Jagger had reconciled, I wasn't sure how Jagger would react to our presence in the club. "I just saw . . ." I began. "I mean, I think I saw . . ."

"Saw what?"

"I just saw Jagger!"

Alexander paused. "Here, in the club?"

I nodded. "When I visited Hipsterville a few months ago, I first encountered Jagger sitting in the balcony when I thought Romeo was leading me to you. That's where Jagger is right now."

"What's he doing up there?" Alexander asked.

"I was afraid if I told you Jagger was above us on the balcony, you'd never come back to Dullsville. But if he saw you dancing here when he thinks you've left town, I don't know what would happen."

Alexander led me back underneath the balcony and leaned against one of its pillars.

"It's okay," he said, brushing my sticky hair away from my face. "I'll go back to Dullsville whether Jagger is here or in Romania."

I lit up. "Really?"

"You have my word."

I pulled him into me, my fingers wrapped around his T-shirt, and kissed him with all my might. I stared into his dark eyes. Maybe it was time to tell Alexander about the real Coffin Club. "I have something to tell you."

"I do, too. I'd rather Jagger not know I'm here."

"But after all you've done for his family. The least he could do is buy you a drink. I really need to—"

"Let's not tempt fate. It's best that he thinks I'm back in Dullsville."

"Uh . . . okay."

"Now, what were you going to tell me?"

"It's time for another dance."

After Alexander gave me a kiss good night outside Aunt Libby's apartment, he admitted he had prior plans with Jameson and wouldn't be able to meet the following evening. I was disappointed, but since I hadn't given Alexander any warning of my arrival in Hipsterville, I tried to be mature. Though I was totally bummed out my boyfriend and I would have a night apart, I hadn't spent any time with Aunt Libby. We were due some family bonding time.

The following day, as usual, I got up late. Fortunately for me, Aunt Libby was not a morning person, either. By the time I woke up and dragged myself out of the cozy confines of her down comforter, I found my aunt wearing a knee-length kimono robe, drinking herbal tea, and listening to NPR.

"It's after two," I said, noticing her stove clock. I was

shocked I'd slept as long as I did but even more surprised that my aunt was still not dressed.

"Well, you had a particularly long day yesterday. And I chose to have a lazy day, too."

Aunt Libby poured me a cup of coffee and fixed me a veggie sandwich.

"I have the perfect place to take you tonight," she said, placing the plate in front of me.

"You don't have a hot date tonight with Devon?" I teased.

"Not until tomorrow night. And I told him you were coming with me."

"Not on your life!"

"Sorry, but he's taking us both to the Summer Arts Festival."

"Well, you have twenty-four hours to convince me that that is a good idea," I said between bites. "So what are we going to do?"

"There's a club here in town that has teen night from nine until eleven."

I rolled my eyes. I imagined a Chuck E. Cheese's with a disco ball.

"It's called the Coffin Club," my aunt exclaimed.

"Excuse me?"

"It has your name written all over it. I don't mean the coffin part, of course. But it's very goth and I think you'd enjoy it."

"I'd love to go!"

"I'm a bit old to be hanging out there, but hey, why not?"

That's why Aunt Libby was so special—she didn't care what people thought. Ever since I was a little girl, my aunt marched to her own drum, African or not.

"So we have a few hours to find something appropriate for me to wear," my aunt stated. "I don't have anything darker than yellow."

Whatever my Aunt Libby did, whether it was drumming so hard she got calluses or performing so much she lost her voice, she put forth 110 percent. Hanging out at a nightclub with her sixteen-year-old niece was no exception.

"Where are we going?" I asked as we hopped into her car. "Hot Gothics?"

Aunt Libby let out a loud laugh. "I have to find something that I can fit into, right?"

A few minutes later, we were driving into a gravel parking lot and walking up the stairs of the vacant elementary school, which was now home to the Village Players Theater.

Along with a car key, mailbox key, building key, and door key, my aunt possessed a Village Players Theater key. It took her a minute or two to figure out which key opened the front entrance door, but she eventually found it.

We sauntered down the main hallway, passing Village Players posters of *West Side Story*, *The Sound of Music*, and

South Pacific, an empty principal's office, and a cafeteria.

We passed a tween-sized water fountain, which still had a wooden step stool placed before it, and stopped in front of a door marked "3." What was once a classroom for ten-year-olds now had a sign above it that read: COSTUME SHOPPE.

The blackboard and filing cabinets were still in place, but the teacher's and child-sized desks had been removed, perhaps sold at an auction or sent over to the new elementary school. Dozens of boxes, labeled BROACHES, HATS, SCARVES, sat on the floor in the front of the classroom, while racks of dusty costumes were lined in rows where the students' desks once belonged.

The room was filled with the combined scents of thrift store clothes and textbooks.

Aunt Libby and I stepped over boxes and dug our way through the old clothes with the sole purpose of bringing out my aunt's inner goth.

"This is so awesome," I said as I began looking through a rack of clothes. "I don't know anyone else who would do this for me."

"Are you kidding? I live for this stuff." My aunt beamed as she sifted through a rack of dresses. "That's one of the reasons why I love acting. I can always wear a different style than what I'd normally wear. I've been stuck in the same look for decades."

"I couldn't imagine you any other way. The way you dress is who you are. It's more than beads and bangles. You aren't doing it to be like someone else, or fit in."

"I gave up fitting in years ago," my aunt said with a laugh.

"That's what my mother doesn't understand about my lipstick and dark clothes. I don't wear tattoos to freak her out; I wear them because I have to. It's me."

Aunt Libby paused.

"My mother never understood my inner style, either," she confessed. "That's what it is, really," she said wisely. "It's not about designers or labels but about self-expression. And attitude."

I smiled inside as well as on the outside. Aunt Libby and I dressed as differently as day and night, but we shared the same values.

"It took me years to figure out who I was," she said. "But really, I've always known who I was, since I was your age. It was just that so many people around me wanted me to be like them and tormented me when I wasn't. Your dad grew up and blended in nicely with the establishment. But I always kept my hippie beads, Pink Floyd albums, and left-of-center ideas. I eventually found people who dug me the way I am."

"That's why it's so cool and meaningful to me for you to change your image for one night on the town together."

"Well, now we'll be more alike than ever." My aunt smiled.

"Here's a black corset," I said, taking a costume off the rack.

"I wore that in *A Midsummer Night's Dream* when I

played Helena," my aunt gushed. "I couldn't breathe for a week."

"How about this?" she asked, modeling a witch's hat presumably from an over-the-top production of *The Wizard of Oz*.

"I think it might be a little overkill," I offered.

Aunt Libby found a Puritanical high-collared black dress. "We wore these in *The Crucible*. If I hike it up a few inches . . . it might be quite fabulous."

"I think it would be ghastly," I complimented her.

Cardboard boxes marked MEN'S, WOMEN'S, and CHILDREN'S lined the wall underneath the windows.

I removed a box from the top of the stack labeled WOMEN'S, 9 and sifted through it. The box was full of everything from cowboy boots to tap shoes, galoshes to stilettos.

"Here's some Mary Janes. With a pair of black tights and that *Crucible* dress, you'll look like . . ."

"A grown-up Wednesday Addams," my aunt said half-heartedly.

"Perfect!" I declared enthusiastically.

Now was time for a Raven Madison Extreme Dream Makeover. The closest I'd ever gotten to being a fashion or cosmetics consultant was when I applied pink blush to Becky when she was preparing for a date with Matt.

If I ever had my own style show, I'd tear into a suburban style-challenged participant's closet and throw out anything pastel, floral, or rhinestoned and replace it with bloodred tones, acid hues, and morbid blacks.

Today was different from anything I'd experienced when consulting Becky. From her auburn-topped head to her lime-green-painted toes, I got to transform my aunt from a flower child to a lady of the night.

While one hand soaked in lavender water, I painted her other hand's fingernails bat black.

"So, tell me all about the date!" I prompted her like a professional cosmetologist.

Aunt Libby giggled as if we were best friends as she described her dinner date with Devon.

"He is unlike any other man I've ever met. He's very patient and intense. He listens to everything I say."

"Do you have a picture of him?"

"We've only had one date. Besides, he doesn't like to have his picture taken."

Curious, I thought. While Aunt Libby's nails were drying, I toned down her warm glow and sun-kissed face by applying a soft, pale white powder. I drew her heavy eyeliner to a point and spread coffin black eyeshadow on her lids. I overapplied her mascara and finished off with two-tone vampire red matte lipstick.

I dolled her up with a hemlock lace choker necklace, rose dangle earrings, and chunky black bracelets. Then I zipped her into her recently hemmed *Crucible* dress.

I quickly unpacked my clubbing clothes and felt like I spent more time getting ready in my aunt's bedroom than riding the bus to Hipsterville.

"I think I'm melting out here," she hollered, knocking

on the bedroom door. "Hurry, I want to see what I look like, too."

I sprayed my hair and opened the door.

"Wow! Get a load of you!" she exclaimed.

I twirled like a model in front of her, wearing a black minidress with a violet and black stretch bodice and jagged skirt, midnight-colored fishnets, and Demonia black leather buckled-up monster boots. I felt confident in my skin and clothes. I'd passed for a vampire in the Dungeon and a young adult in the Coffin Club and I was just being myself. It was electrifying that I had the opportunity to return as myself—much less with my aunt Libby.

Only she didn't think so. "Next to you I look like I could be your grandmother!"

"Get out! We look like sisters."

"As long as you give me props like that, I'll hang out with you wherever you want. Where to next, the cemetery?"

"Now, are you ready to see yourself?" I asked.

"For like an hour. . . ."

"Drumroll please . . ." I began, and presented her in front of her full-length bedroom mirror.

When my aunt saw her reflected image, she didn't recognize herself. She gasped as if she'd just seen a ghost.

"You look beautiful, don't you think?" I beamed.

"Well . . . it's certainly different from what I'm used to."

"I made you look like me," I said with admiration.

There was dead silence. Then, as if she thought she'd hurt my feelings, she said, "No one can look like you, Raven. You are unique and beautiful."

"I can tone it down."

"Don't you dare." She grabbed a handheld mirror and fluffed her hair. "This color is very slimming." She puckered her vampire red lips like a morbid Marilyn Monroe. "Black is a girl's best friend."

9

Ghouls' Night Out

"Look at that line!" Aunt Libby shrieked when we arrived at the Coffin Club. "It's as long as a New York hot spot's! This will not do—follow me."

Aunt Libby headed straight for the entrance and right up to an unfamiliar bouncer.

"Excuse me, my name is Libby Madison. I'm with the Village Players and . . ."

"Libby?" the bouncer asked skeptically.

My aunt scrutinized him. "Jake?" she asked, suddenly recognizing him. "What are you doing working here?"

"It's just part-time while I go to school," he said, taking the five-dollar teen-night admission fee from a girl in line. "I almost didn't recognize you."

"Well, I'm out clubbing tonight. Do I look the part?"

Jake smiled and stamped a fourteen-year-old who had

more piercings than I had. The stamp barely fit on her tiny hand.

"Raven, this is Jake," my aunt began proudly. "Jake, this is my niece, Raven. Jake played Lenny in the Village Players production of *Of Mice and Men*."

"It's nice to meet you." He stamped a bat on each of our hands.

"Don't we need bracelets?" I asked.

"Not tonight. The bar is dry until eleven oh one."

"How did you know about the bracelets?" my aunt whispered.

"Uh . . . I saw it in a movie."

Jake hopped off his stool and, like the valet at a five-star hotel, kindly opened the coffin-shaped doors.

My aunt and I paraded through the doors like we were royalty.

"When I grow up, Aunt Libby, I want to be just like you!" I exclaimed.

My aunt took a moment to take in the Coffin Club, beginning with its neon tombstones.

"I love it!" she blurted out.

I, however, was taken aback. The mood of the club had totally changed from the previous nights I'd visited. It was like a cryptic sweet-sixteen party. No amount of white powder or Graveyard Gray lipstick could hide the pimples, braces, and bubble gum attached to the teens running amok throughout the club. Sure, some teens were bopping to the macabre music or experimenting with a darker fashion palette, but for most it seemed a chance to be away from Mommy and Daddy and play dress-up for the evening.

Aunt Libby couldn't have cared less, even if she'd known. She was absorbing her surroundings like a tan addict enjoys the sun.

"This club is amazing!" she said. "I didn't realize there were so many of you."

"Neither did I," I said.

"Who is this singing?" she asked, swaying to the music.

"The Skeletons."

"I'll have to get this album," she said. "I mean download it. Whatever."

As we made our way farther into the club, I did notice an older group of goths dancing and partying. They, like me, seemed to gaze at the younger set with disdain. Perhaps I should have been more open-minded.

"I want to quench my thirst," my aunt said when she spotted the spiderwebbed, bottled bar.

"Sure. My treat," I offered.

"Absolutely not."

The same woman from last night waited on us.

"Hey, didn't I see you before?"

"Uh . . . no."

"I swear I saw you in here last night."

"I'm afraid not."

"You were here with your boyfriend. He's tall and really hot."

"It wasn't us."

"Sadly she was at home," my aunt confessed. "I had her chained in all night."

"Well, you must have one of those faces."

"My niece? She's as original as they come."

My aunt read the virgin drink specials, etched out on a gravestone next to the cash register.

"We'd like two Insane Asylums, please. No alcohol."

"That's all we're serving tonight. We don't make much at the bar on teen night."

"Well, we'll remember that when we leave a tip," my aunt said. "I was a waitress for longer than I care to tell you. I understand completely."

Aunt Libby had a way of talking to anyone like a friend.

Just then I spotted Romeo out of my peripheral vision.

He came over to get some cherries from the plastic condiments container in front of me.

I ducked, hiding my face by rooting around aimlessly in my purse.

"He's cute," my aunt said, nudging me.

"Aunt Libby!" I said.

"Don't be shy. But what am I telling you for? You've got a boyfriend. By the way, when am I going to meet this Alexander Sterling?"

"Shhh!"

"What. Did I say something wrong?"

Romeo stopped in front of us. He pointed his finger

at me as if trying to remember my name.

"Didn't I see you . . . ?"

"You have her confused with someone else," Aunt Libby said. "C'mon, let's dance."

And with that we finished our drinks and hit the dance floor.

I was surprised that Aunt Libby danced as well as she did. But after all, she was an actress and spent most of her life onstage. I'm sure she had to tap, twirl, and jitterbug her way through various parts in her career. The Coffin Club's dance floor was just an extension of my aunt's performance art, and she was rocking as if she were dancing for an audience of thousands.

Aunt Libby was exhausted before I was and asked if we could take a break. We sat for a few moments on the coffin-shaped couches, catching our breath, then hit the mini–flea market on the other side of the club. Aunt Libby was in artsy heaven. She didn't know which seller or reader to approach first.

"Let's buy you some jewelry." Aunt Libby cased the rows of rings, pendants, bracelets made from pewter, crystals, and beads.

"You don't have to buy me anything."

"But I want to . . . I'm your aunt. Everything here is handmade. Pick something you like."

A bracelet did catch my eye. It was a skinny beaded bracelet with a charm—a petite bottle of love potion.

I placed it on my arm, along with my hidden plastic club bracelet, and gave my aunt a huge "Thank you" squeeze.

Then something caught her eye. "Tarot cards!" she exclaimed. "Let's get our cards read."

"Sounds like a great idea. You go first."

When my aunt sat down, I realized that this was my chance to revisit the underground club. I hated to ditch her, especially after she'd just bought me a special gift, but it would only be for a few minutes—no more time than it would take to go to a crowded restroom and back. I knew if I ever wanted to see the club again, this was my only chance. The secret door was hiding somewhere in close proximity and I had to investigate the club further. It would take only a few minutes, and by the time my aunt finished having her future and past lives read, I'd have already returned.

"I have to go the ghouls room. Don't worry if I'm gone for a few. These drinks go right through me."

Aunt Libby wasn't bothered. She'd already begun talking to the spiritually gifted woman as if she were her long-time therapist.

I tried to retrace my steps the night I'd stumbled upon the hidden entrance. I was heading for the ghouls room when I'd become distracted from the dry-ice fog. I stood near the bar, closed my eyes, and spun around, trying to disorient myself. Then I pushed through the teens and headed for the ghouls room. When I discovered I was heading in the opposite direction, I figured I was on target. I saw a wall obscured by the shadows. I slid my hand along it, combing the pine for the secret door, when I found what appeared to be a broom closet. Bull's-eye.

I turned the knob of the small coffin-shaped door and pushed with all my might. When it opened into a darkened corridor, I knew I'd found my way. I quickly followed the narrow hallway and hurried down the plunging staircase. When I reached the coffin lid marked DEAD END I tried to push it open.

Of course, I found it locked.

I didn't have a choice. I knocked.

I banged and banged, but no one answered. I paced for a moment, hoping someone would soon descend the staircase. But when a few minutes went by and I remained alone, I became antsy.

I imagined Onyx and Scarlet kicking it up on the dance floor, drinking bloody drinks and gossiping about their nightlife activities. My new vampire buddies, Onyx and Scarlet. Why hadn't I thought of them sooner?

I grabbed my cell from my purse. I scrolled through my Friends List until it hit Scarlet, then I pressed the Send button.

I waited for a moment for the phone to connect. There was so much concrete and stone surrounding me, it was impossible to get a signal. I raced back up the staircase and pressed the Send button again. Ring . . . Ring . . . Ring . . .

"Come on, Scarlet," I said to myself. "Pick up." I was sure she wouldn't be able to hear the phone above the club music. I was just a coffin lid away from being back into the vampire club of my dreams.

"Hello?" a girl's voice answered.

"Scarlet?" I asked excitedly.

"Yes?"

"It's Raven."

"Raven. What's going on?"

"I'm right outside the Dungeon door. I forgot my key."

"I'll be there in a sec."

A few moments later, the door creaked open and Onyx and Scarlet were standing behind the medieval-looking Dragon.

Each girl took me by the hand and led me through the slit in the curtain, past the crowded bar, and out onto the dance floor.

Strangely, the already dangerous and otherworldly underground club now seethed with tension. The clubsters who once appeared seductive and inviting now eyed one another skeptically, whispering in private meetings.

Onyx and Scarlet, however, seemed unchanged. Scarlet placed a skeleton key in my hand and closed my fingers shut.

"This way you'll never be locked out," she said.

"But—"

"No need to argue—we're here all the time."

"And when we aren't here, we're together," Onyx added.

I placed my new prized possession in my purse before they changed their mind.

"We were hoping you would come," Onyx said, leading me to the bar. "Want some refreshment? Tonight is buy one, get one free."

"No thanks," I said.

My fantasy was to be a vampire—to live the immortal life, be seduced by the night, to love Alexander for eternity. What I hadn't envisioned was guzzling down a goblet filled with blood as if it were chocolate milk. "I can't stay long tonight, but I wanted to pop in and say hello."

"We're so glad you did," Scarlet said. "So much is happening." Arm in arm, we zigzagged through the catacombs. I tried to remember which path we were taking by making mental notes of the landmarks in the tunnels. We passed a girl bridled with passion, leaning against a tomb, her date kissing her on the neck. A few dozen skulls lined the walls. A group of clubsters were lying in some of the hollowed graves. Then I was distracted as Onyx began to ask me questions.

"How was your date last night?" she probed.

"Uh . . . great."

We passed an enigmatic figure lurking in the shadows. A few votives lining the floor in an adjacent alcove next to the mysterious person cast a speck of light on a pair of motorcycle boots.

I glanced back as we continued to walk ahead. The figure remained hidden in the shadows.

We ducked underneath a sunken archway and entered a lounge called Torture Chamber. An electric chair, a rack, and a stockade were prominently displayed there. A huge circular wooden platform with half a dozen tables on it revolved ever so slowly. A freestanding bar, the size found at a wedding reception, was off to the side. We sat down at the only unoccupied table.

"Why don't you bring your boyfriend here?" Scarlet asked.

"I'm not sure if he would like this club."

"Is he a mortal?" Onyx inquired.

The two girls waited on edge for my response. But it was I who was most anxiously awaiting the words to flow from my lips. "No, my boyfriend is not a mortal. He is a vampire," I said. It was the first time I'd ever admitted that my boyfriend was immortal (except once to Becky and she thought I was trying to make her laugh). I felt as if a burden had been lifted from my shoulders, and it was exhilarating. "My boyfriend is a vampire," I repeated proudly.

"Then you have to bring him here," Onyx suggested. "The whole point of this club is for us to have a place we can call our own."

"And that might change," Scarlet said secretively.

"Why?" I asked.

"We've heard rumblings that someone is planning to take over the club."

One person—who I'd seen having secret meetings— sprang to mind. I remembered Phoenix talking to his henchmen. He was magnetically alluring and mysteriously dangerous. I could see his followers heeding his every command. "Phoenix—," I said in a whisper.

"What?" Scarlet asked. "I can't hear you above the music."

I felt the hairs on the ends of my neck stand up. I

glanced back and Phoenix was sitting in the electric chair, staring right at me.

My heart sank to my stomach. Though I was surrounded by two friendly vampires, I was deathly afraid of the one behind me.

"Never mind," I said. Even though he was out of earshot and the club music was pulsing faster than my beating heart, I sensed he could hear every word.

"The club has been a great hangout," Scarlet began.

"The whole reason the club exists is so that we can be ourselves peacefully," Onyx said.

"There are many of us who don't want a new direction. The club is being torn apart," Scarlet admitted, shaking her head.

I had to know more. I leaned into the girls as closely as I could. "What's his story?" I whispered to Onyx.

"Whose story?" She scooted closer.

"What?" Scarlet asked, tossing her luscious locks over her shoulder. "I can't hear you."

"She's interested in some guy," Onyx said.

"I thought you had a boyfriend," Scarlet added.

Onyx nudged her best friend, then eagerly asked me, "Which one?"

I placed my index finger over my lips. In my softest whisper I began, "I'm not interested . . . I mean I am . . . but not that way. Don't look now . . . but the guy behind me, sitting in the electric chair . . ."

Onyx did her best to check him out without being too noticeable, but Scarlet glared toward the stockade. "Who, him? That's the bartender."

I shook my head. "No, not him."

"No, she means over there," Onyx corrected. "But there's no one in or near the electric chair."

I spun around. The electric chair was empty.

"Who were you interested in?" Scarlet asked.

"Uh . . . no one really."

"Tell us," Onyx pried.

"The biker dude with purple hair," I confessed.

"He's your type, huh?" Onyx continued. "Hot, mysterious, and dangerous?"

"No—I have a boyfriend. It just seems he's always hiding in the shadows and watching me."

"I haven't gotten the scoop on him yet. But I'd stay away," Scarlet warned.

"Yeah, he's always having meetings with really gnarly types," Onyx confirmed. "Maybe he's the one—"

The bartender approached our table with a tray of three red martinis.

"We didn't order these," Scarlet said.

"They are from the two guys sitting in the corner," the waiter stated.

The two guys who'd let me in the Dungeon a few nights before raised their goblets to us.

"Two dudes for three girls? How obnoxious," Scarlet remarked.

"It's okay. I have a boyfriend," I said.

"But it's the point," she charged. "They don't know that."

"I've heard if you accept a stranger's drink, then it's an invitation to your table," I whispered to the girls. "Thanks anyway," I said to the bartender, declining the martini.

"I never refuse a free drink," Onyx said. The two girls laughed and gladly accepted the bloody drinks.

But I wasn't interested in freebies. I wanted the scoop about the inner workings of the club.

"So will the club close?" I asked.

"We hope not!" Onyx began, drawing near. "We've met so many fabulous people here."

"And where else could we hang out and be ourselves? A coffee shop?"

"They certainly don't sell AB-negative lattes." Both girls laughed.

Scarlet scooted close. "Do you know Jagger Maxwell?"

I nodded. "He's legendary. What about him?"

"Since he opened this club a few months ago, he created a safe haven for us to be ourselves and party," Scarlet said in a whisper.

"He even gave all the out-of-town members a place to crash here," said Onyx.

"But now that's not good enough for some," Scarlet added. "So the buzz is that Jagger has another plan."

"He doesn't want us to be a secret," Onyx said.

"But that will blow the whole purpose of the Dungeon," Scarlet continued.

"To be visible—but only to us immortals."

"Jagger and his crew think that it's a vampire's true nature to lurk among the mortals."

"So many of us believe just the opposite. It's best to keep our blood pure and separate from mortals."

"If we reveal our true identity," Scarlet warned, "then we obviously pose as much of a threat to mortals as they do to us."

"Jagger is on a power trip. He wasn't happy enough being the leader of the Dungeon. He doesn't have our best interest in mind. He has his own."

"What do you believe? What kind of vampire are you?" Onyx asked with conviction.

I was taken aback. Two vampiresses, one flashing an onyx on her fang, were asking me what kind of vampire I was? I certainly couldn't say that I was neither kind—and in fact, not a vampire at all.

"We should remain private and pure," I answered emphatically. "In the end, will mortals really accept us as we are? I think it's best we remain true to ourselves so we don't lose our identity. We are who we are for a reason. We don't fit into their world, so why should we try?"

I was talking as much about vampires as I was about myself.

The girls grinned in agreement.

We sensed someone listening to our conversation. We peered up and the two guys were standing behind us.

"See," I said through a fake smile.

"Do you mind if we sit down?" the blond asked.

"Of course not," Scarlet said.

It was then I spotted tousled dark purple hair in the chamber across from us.

"Uh . . . I'm feeling dizzy," I admitted, referring to the revolving floor. "I'll be right back."

It was my chance to spy on Phoenix. I snuck out into the hall and hid in the shadows next to their lounge.

Phoenix, along with a gang of ominous-looking guys, was hovering around a stone table. Phoenix was quite popular. When he wasn't slinking in the shadows, he was surrounded by club members. "Jagger doesn't know the true meaning of being a vampire," one said.

"It's time he steps down," added another.

"And you are just the dude to take over," the first one said to Phoenix.

"Yes," they all said in unison.

"Tomorrow night, then," a voice declared.

"I'll meet him at the crop circle. It will be done," Phoenix finished.

I leaned back as far as I could into the shadows as Phoenix left the chamber and the menacing clubsters followed him.

Phoenix was planning a revolt of his own. What would happen if he led the vampire club? Was he the kind of vampire who thought it necessary to lurk among the mortals? If he was planning to meet Jagger in the open, he was surely risking exposure himself.

I felt a vibration in my purse. I pulled out my cell. It was Aunt Libby.

"Raven? Where are you?" she asked, her voice concerned. "I just checked the ghouls room and you weren't there."

"I took a wrong turn. I'm a few yards from the dance floor," I said truthfully, only it wasn't the same dance floor she was thinking of.

"I'm done with my reading. She said marriage is in the cards."

"I'll meet you at the tarot card booth."

I hung up. If the tarot card reader had been truly psychic, she would have informed my aunt of my real location. Fortunately her powers were really only good for taking other people's money.

I returned to find the girls still immersed in cozy conversation with the martini guys.

"Where did you go?" Onyx said.

"I got turned around. Even a ghost could get lost in these tombs." The blond beamed. A tiny drop of blood dripped from the corner of his mouth. Onyx wiped it off with her martini napkin.

"I really have to go."

"So soon?" Scarlet asked.

"Yes, I have to get back."

"You'll have to join us tomorrow," Onyx said, entwined with the redheaded guy.

"Yeah, you'll have to join us," he repeated.

I set off on my quest to meet Aunt Libby. Once again, I was lost in the tombs. I didn't remember which way Onyx, Scarlet, and I had entered or how far we'd walked. I couldn't find the embedded skulls, or the clubsters hanging out in the hallowed graves. And there were dozens of girls in the labyrinth of tunnels with guys hanging from their necks.

I entered an alcove filled with gamers playing Medieval Morticians, another with members having black widow races, and still another playing Spin the Bloody Bottle. All were dead ends.

I was so lost I was ready to scream. I had to get back to Aunt Libby before she got worried and called the cops or, worse, my parents. At the end of one catacomb, I discovered a door. I hoped it led to the outside of the club and I'd head back through the main entrance. There wasn't a knob anywhere to be found. In the darkness, I glided my hand along the unstained wood until I discovered a latch. I squeezed it and slid it open. The door didn't exit into an alleyway but rather into someone's apartment—a loft with dozens of medieval candelabras. For a moment I paused. Something looked familiar about it, and then I realized I'd been here before. It was Jagger's apartment.

I snuck inside, wondering what insights I might gain this time from the threatening vampire.

The gray metal main door on the opposite side was open overhead. An aquarium, empty of water but filled with rocks and one deadly tarantula, remained near the radiator, as I'd remembered.

In the far corner of the loft lay a coffin, adorned with gothic band stickers, encircled by dirt.

I noticed a wooden stake caked with mud and grass, a spool of rope, and several long boards—similar to the tools I'd seen on a TV show about making a homemade crop circle.

I sensed someone lingering at the door behind me. I slowly turned around.

It was Phoenix. His sunglasses cast a shadow on his pale face, making it difficult to see his expression.

"What is it you are looking for?" he asked in his thick Romanian accent.

I felt alarmed. I knew I wasn't supposed to be nosing around Jagger's apartment, or the Dungeon, for that matter. Phoenix appeared to be watching me, always in the background, showing up unexpectedly in a blanket of darkness. My not knowing his motives made him especially intriguing and suspicious.

"You shouldn't be snooping around. I can escort you out."

"That won't be necessary," I heard someone say from the other side of the room. Jagger was standing at the apartment's main entrance. "Raven is an old friend. And I've known her boyfriend for an eternity."

Both vampires were blocking the exits—the one that led back to the club and the one that led to a hallway. (I'd remembered coming down the dimly lit corridor when I first visited Jagger's apartment.) The room was windowless and there were no other exits. I had no way to escape.

I didn't know which vampire to side with. I wasn't fast enough to whisk by them or strong enough to bulldoze through them. Either one could easily tear into my flesh with a single bite.

I did something I never thought I'd do. I tore off and hid behind Jagger Maxwell.

I chose the company of the nefarious but familiar Jagger to the foreign leather-clad stranger.

"She has such good taste," he said brazenly to Phoenix. And with that Jagger shut the door to his apartment and to Phoenix.

I wasn't sure why Jagger was being nice to me. Perhaps he felt he had an obligation to Alexander since he'd returned his sibling safely to him. But ultimately Jagger was untrustworthy. It was only a matter of time before Jagger flashed his fangs or verbally threatened me as I followed him down the dimly lit corridor to a freight elevator. But instead of challenging me, Jagger calmly led me through the desolate hallway, without incident, like a knight guarding its queen. I was shocked. He was honoring his truce with Alexander. Apparently their reconciliation was as meaningful to him as it had been to my boyfriend. I was almost disappointed when I got inside the elevator, alone, without having been confronted. I guess I had made the right choice after all. Still standing in the hallway, Jagger began to shut the rickety door. As it creaked closed, something swooped underneath and fluttered so close above my head, I had to duck.

When I recovered, I noticed a bat hanging upside down from the ceiling. Its beady black eyes were looking dead straight at me.

A single bulb illuminated the elevator like a B horror flick. I quickly pressed a button marked "C.C."

Jagger glared back at me with his mismatched mesmerizing eyes. "I hope you enjoyed your visit. You never know. You may want to join forever," he said with a wicked grin.

The elevator screeched as it slowly ascended from the depths of the Dungeon to club level and then ground to a stop.

I quickly opened the heavy elevator door and spotted the indoor entrance to the Coffin Club. I made my way inside just as the bat flew off overhead.

Safely back at Aunt Libby's apartment, I sat up on her futon and scribbled in my journal, the streetlight casting a glow on my comforter. My aunt was fast asleep, but I felt like I'd just guzzled an extra-tall chocolate toffee latte.

I had so many quandaries buzzing through my mind. I wasn't sure why I was pulled toward Phoenix, just as I'd been to Trevor and Jagger. It wasn't the same way I'd been attracted to Alexander, but Phoenix sparked my curiosity, and I was intrigued to know why he was similarly drawn to me. I was also worried about the situation of the club. If Phoenix took over, what would that mean for my new friends? The girls might have a secure place for all eternity—safe and free from the possible persecution of mortals. With Jagger in charge, would it mean that Hipsterville would have a known vampire presence? It irked me that Jagger was so power hungry that he would risk the welfare of his own kind. His actions went against everything Alexander believed in. Alexander wanted to blend in the mortal world as mortal, while Jagger wanted to be feared by others—to gain popularity and notoriety. I understood Jagger's yearning to be known. It wasn't in my nature to remain hidden in the shadows—but there was one big difference—I wasn't a vampire. I wasn't a danger to anyone. And since I was beginning to immerse myself in a community of vampires—the life I'd always dreamed of—I had to wonder if this new world was that different from the world I already belonged to. The Dungeon was being pulled in two directions, just like any mortal community. Mortals and immortals might not be that different after all.

But I had to admit, the immortal world was intoxicating to me. It had all the draws of the mortal world, with the edge and darkness that I so desired. Though I couldn't completely shake off that dream I'd had a few nights ago. At this point, I had the best of both worlds. I didn't have to make a decision to become anything different from what I already was. Even though it was under false pretenses, I was accepted into the Dungeon as myself. If that changed, I wasn't sure the Underworld would be so enticing after all.

All of Hipsterville was asleep except for those clubsters in the Dungeon, dancing and drinking, and one lone vampire, Alexander Sterling. I missed him and hated that I was unable to be by his side throughout his long nights. I hungered for Alexander to hold me safely in the warm night air, underneath the moonlight by tombstones in a far-off cemetery, naive to the troubles of the underground vampires. I dreamed of a time before I knew of the Dungeon, Jagger, or Phoenix.

Wasn't it enough just to deal with the trials and tribulations of dating a vampire?

I had one mission when summer break began—to see Alexander. But once again, my curiosity had led me off my path and straight into a labyrinth of danger.

I was learning even more about Alexander's complicated world—without him.

10

Picture Perfect

The Hipsterville Art Festival, according to Aunt Libby, was an event showcasing regional artisans dating back to the founding of the town. It was quite a to-do. Five blocks of Main Street, with its quaint boutiques and coffee shops, were cordoned off, allowing patrons and sellers to walk freely in the road without fear of being run over by an old Accord covered with DAVE MATTHEWS, SAVE THE RAIN FOREST, and PETA stickers. Sellers traveled in from neighboring states to peddle their original handcrafted wares. Bright blue and red booths lined the streets, displaying and selling everything from pottery to purses. The early-evening fresh air smelled deliciously of sizzling steak, barbecue, and grilled corn on the cob. Kids enjoyed face painting while adults entered raffles to win prizes from microwaves to a brand-new car.

At the north end of the festival, a jazz band played by

a fountain with a statue of the town founder. Elderly and young Hipstervillians alike relaxed in sun chairs, tapping their feet to the lively tunes.

Normally, Aunt Libby was known to be late to every event, dinner, or meeting. Tonight, she was so excited to see her new beau, she was showered, dressed, redressed, and ready to go an hour before our scheduled meeting— at the fountain just after sunset. Not only was I eager to see Alexander, I was going on a double date with adults. Aunt Libby and I anxiously waited by the jazz band for our dates to arrive.

"I can't wait for you to meet Alexander," I exclaimed to my aunt.

"Me too," she said, giving me a familial squeeze. "I'm looking forward to seeing what you think of Devon. I want your honest opinion. I haven't been the greatest judge of character in my life. However, I think this one is a keeper."

Aunt Libby kept a rhythmic beat by shaking her hips, her floral sundress flowing and her dangling earrings swinging. If I'd been standing by my mother, I would have been horrified. But I was excited to see my aunt so free-spirited and happy, and I found myself unexpectedly rocking.

The sun seemed to be still over the bell tower in the distance.

"I wonder if I jumped up and down if it would make the sun set any faster," I said to my aunt.

I scanned the festival crowd, filled with hipsters, granola heads, goths. Couples of all ages, shapes, and sizes were milling about. Children running, holding balloons, or being pushed in strollers were enjoying the fair.

I glanced among the eclectic crowd, imagining Alexander thriving in the sunlight instead of the moonlight. I watched several cozy couples, hand in hand, wishing it could be Alexander and me.

Before I knew it, dusk had overtaken Main Street. The gaslights illuminated the streets like nineteenth-century London. I remarked to Aunt Libby how lucky we were that the rainy days had departed and the clouds had disappeared for the night of the festival.

A handsome man with two cotton candies (one pastel pink, the other baby blue) appeared out of the crowd and approached us. My aunt was helping a toddler reshape his balloon animal and was unaware a man was standing by our side.

"You must be Raven," he said. Aunt Libby's ears perked up and she swung around.

"Devon!" my aunt called, returning the animal to the toddler.

Devon was a dashing older gentleman with graying hair and a square jawline. He had piercing eyes and wore designer jeans, Bjorn sandals, a linen sport coat, and a gold earring. He appeared lean and fit, like he spent most of his days jogging to Wild Oats.

My aunt, powerful and independent, appeared to turn to mush in Devon's presence. She seemed to be entranced by him, just like an unsuspecting audience member is riveted by a hypnotist.

Then I began to question . . . no, he couldn't be . . . The spell he had my aunt under—was it love or something more Underworldly? After all, Hipsterville was experiencing an increasing population of vampires. And he was unusually pale for an earthy-crunchy type and happened to show up just after sunset.

Someone tapped me on the shoulder.

I turned around and saw my favorite Nosferatu.

"Alexander!" I wrapped my arms around him and gave him a tight squeeze.

I wanted Alexander to dip me back and press his fang-filled mouth on my neck, but instead he gave me a quick kiss on the cheek—an appropriate display of affection in front of my aunt and her date.

"I'd like you to meet Alexander. This is my aunt Libby and Devon." I was so proud to show him off to my aunt. She'd never known me to have a boyfriend, since I never had one. I suddenly felt grown up.

"He's so adorable!" Aunt Libby gushed as if Alexander weren't standing right in front of her.

"You are even more beautiful in person," Alexander kindly complimented her.

The two men shook hands and I watched them closely. I had my suspicions about Devon, and I wondered if I could sense anything by their interaction. But there was nothing unusual in their introduction.

The four of us set out to stroll through the festival. My aunt and I shared our cotton candy with our dates. Alexander and I walked hand in hand while Aunt Libby hung on Devon's every word. We moseyed in and out of the booths, modeling and pointing at anything and everything we fancied.

Two girls, one dressed in a long corset gown, the other in a My Chemical Romance T-shirt, leggings, and checkered flats, entered a booth ahead of us. It was Scarlet and Onyx.

I left Alexander at the pottery booth, approached the girls, and tapped them on the shoulder.

Simultaneously they turned toward me. I realized I didn't have an explanation for Alexander or Aunt Libby as to how I knew these two goth girls. In one moment Onyx and Scarlet would be giving me a huge hug and I would have to explain the origin of our acquaintance. They obviously didn't go to Dullsville High. They weren't distant relatives. And explaining I'd met them at a vampire club was most especially not going to fly.

But when our eyes met, their expressions appeared vacant.

"Have we met?" Scarlet asked.

My heart dropped. I felt the same feeling I had in school when I was five and tried to play kickball with catalogue cutout neighborhood kids and they took the ball from me and went inside. For the last two nights I'd partied with these girls, and we'd instantly bonded like we were old friends. I had clearly been mistaken. Then it hit me. They were fearful of my revealing their identity.

"I thought you were someone else," I said knowingly, but still saddened.

"We get that all the time," Scarlet said.

The girls eyed Alexander, who was now catching up to me.

Onyx gave me a quick wink before they turned and walked away.

"Who was that?" Alexander asked, grabbing my hand.

"I think I saw her at the Coffin Club," I said truthfully.

"Speaking of which, what did you do last night?" he asked.

"Well, you'll never believe it."

"You went to the Coffin Club!" he exclaimed.

"How did you know?" I asked, bewildered.

He pointed to the faded bat on my hand.

"Oh, that . . ." I said.

"Raven, I'd asked you not to go. I don't want to appear like an overprotective boyfriend, but . . . Promise me you won't go back."

"It's not as sinister as it sounds," I defended. "I went with Aunt Libby. In fact, it was her idea."

Alexander seemed surprised yet relieved.

"Did I hear someone say 'the Coffin Club?'" My aunt, a few feet away from us, spun around and proudly displayed her black fingernails. "We had the best time ever! We drank Insane Asylums. I felt at least ten years younger."

Alexander smiled. I could tell he was imagining my aunt trying to conjure up ghosts at the bar.

"Maybe we should go," my aunt suggested to Devon. "Have you been?"

I waited desperately for Devon's answer. Though he was older than the combined ages of two average clubsters at the nightspot, I wouldn't have been surprised if he'd checked it out.

I was intrigued to hear his response.

"There's supposed to be an underground club inside. A real vampire hangout." He laughed.

Alexander and I locked eyes.

"We didn't see that when we were there," my aunt admitted. "Sounds like fun."

"It's just something I heard," he said to me.

How would Devon know about the vampire hangout? I could only fathom he must have visited it himself.

We continued on and passed a booth with blown-glass ornaments and figures.

"We'll catch up to you," I called to my aunt, and pulled Alexander inside.

Alexander studied the artisan blowing glass into a tiny elephant.

"I have strong suspicions about Devon," I whispered.

"What do you suspect?" he asked, mesmerized by the flaming torch.

"That he's a . . ." Then I turned his face toward mine and mouthed the word *vampire*.

Alexander laughed and returned to watch the artisan sculpt the tiny trunk.

"It's possible," I persisted.

"Yes it is."

"See? Then you believe me! Devon doesn't like to have

his picture taken, and Aunt Libby says his stares are hypnotic. He didn't show up until after sunset, and now he's talking about vampire clubs."

"So what if he is?"

"Then we have to warn her."

All at once Alexander wasn't interested in the sculpture. "You don't want your aunt dating a vampire?" His midnight eyes couldn't hide the sadness inside him. I was making Alexander feel that same awful feeling I'd felt when Scarlet didn't acknowledge me or when my classmates ostracized me. After all, Alexander was a vampire, and I'd just told him I didn't want my own aunt dating someone of his kind.

"I didn't mean . . ." I said, reaching out to him.

"But you did," he argued flatly.

"No—that's not what I meant." Then I realized I had meant it. My eyes welled up with tears.

Alexander led me away from the crowd and in between two booths. He sidestepped a puddle of Coke while I despondently plunged right into it.

He brushed away a tear that had trickled down my cheek.

"I didn't mean to offend you," I began. "I'd never—"

"I know," he said, then continued in a soft voice. "Raven, you have reason to be concerned. It's not like dating someone outside your religion, class, or comfort zone. Vampires by nature are deadly to mortals. It's what I've been trying to tell you since we met."

"That's why I said what I did. But you aren't like that.

So maybe Devon isn't, either."

"First of all, we don't know what Devon is or isn't."

"If he is and he's like you, then it would be awesome!"

"Or he could be like Jagger. That's why I'm protective of you. Don't you understand?"

"But Alexander, there are vampires who are just like you."

"What do you mean?"

I was ready to tell Alexander everything about the underground club when Aunt Libby interrupted. "You have to see this painting," she said, grabbing my arm. "You won't believe it!"

Unrelentingly she dragged me through the crowd, weaving in and out of festival-goers until we finally stopped at a booth in front of the firehouse.

On an easel, beside a painting of a vase full of flowers, was a picture of *me*. Dressed in my scarlet and black corset prom dress, wearing lace gloves, and carrying a black parasol, I was standing outside the Mansion. Three bats hovered around me—one with green eyes, a smaller one with blue eyes, and one with one blue and one green. Up behind me at the attic window, the curtain was slightly pulled back and a silhouetted figure watched over me.

In the corner of the painting was a big blue ribbon.

"This looks exactly like you!" Aunt Libby remarked.

Devon examined it, then me. "It certainly does."

"It is me!" I exclaimed.

"Who painted this?" Aunt Libby asked the festival volunteer. "We have to find this person."

"There was no information on the artist. Usually they attach a picture, website, and bio. But the artist must have wanted anonymity."

"It looks flawless, like a photograph," my aunt observed.

"We've been getting inquiries and requests to buy it all day."

"You can't sell it," my aunt began, "until we find out more about it."

"It does bear an uncanny resemblance to you," the volunteer commented. "Do you know any artists?"

Devon, my aunt, and the volunteer searched the painting for a signature. I stood in awe while Alexander hung back.

"Here it is!" my aunt exclaimed, like she'd just spotted an egg on an Easter hunt. In the corner, embedded in a spider's web, was the name "Sterling."

"Sterling . . . That's you—," my aunt announced to Alexander.

Devon and the volunteer turned to Alexander.

"This is why you stayed in town?" I asked Alexander.

"Jameson insisted I enter," he said self-consciously.

"That's my niece," my aunt declared proudly. "And her boyfriend is the artist."

"It is sure nice to meet you," the volunteer said as if she were meeting a celebrity. "Here's my card. I know that the curator of a gallery was interested in this piece. If you have others, I'm sure he'd love to see them, too."

"This is why you stayed so long in Hipsterville. You

were preparing to show your artwork in this fair."

Alexander didn't respond.

"Why didn't you tell me?" I asked, squeezing his hand.

"I'm sure there are a lot of things you don't tell me," he said, pointing to the bat stamp on my hand.

A few hours later the annual art festival was coming to a close. Sellers were packing up and booths were being dismantled. The four of us sat at the rim of the fountain, our bellies full of food and our feet tired from walking.

Aunt Libby and Devon sauntered over to a festival exit a few yards away to say good night while Alexander and I cuddled by the waterfall.

"I'll pick you up tomorrow night," Alexander said, his arm around my shoulder. "And I'll have a surprise for you."

"I can't wait. I'll be counting the minutes!"

His face lit up like the moon shining above him.

Alexander leaned into me and gave me a slow kiss. His lips tasted like soda and caramel apples.

He watched me from the fountain as I headed over to my aunt and her boyfriend, who were now holding hands and getting lost in each other's eyes. At any minute, Devon could lean over to her and sink his fangs into her neck—if he had any. But if he did, would he really do it in front of the whole town?

Knowing my aunt Libby, a carefree otherworldly old soul, she might wish to become a vampire. Just my luck, I'd have to visit my aunt in the Underworld while I remained an outsider mortal in Dullsville.

"It was great meeting you, Raven," Devon said when I finally caught up to them.

"Thanks for the cotton candy," I replied. "Hope to see you soon."

I turned away so the new couple would have a private moment before their departure. More important, I had to confirm Devon's true identity.

I got my compact out of my purse, opened it, and angled it behind me. I took a breath when my aunt tapped me on the shoulder. When I glanced into the reflection, Devon had already disappeared.

Aunt Libby and I spent the midnight hours curled up in our pajamas on the futon, as if at a slumber party, surrounded by rose-scented votives and lavender incense and talking incessantly about our gorgeous guys.

My aunt was giddy as she replayed every girlie thought and feeling she had.

"So where will you have your wedding?" I asked as we sipped on chamomile tea.

"I think it's too early to scout locations," she said with a laugh. "But I've always wanted to get married outside."

Then I posed a perfect sleepover-type question. "How far would you go, to show your love for him?"

"Like would I move?" she asked.

That wasn't what I had in mind. "Sure," I said, playing along.

She shrugged her shoulders. "Would I have to work?"

"Uh . . . no," I answered. My aunt was getting further away from the point of my playful interrogation.

"Would I be able to perform full-time?" she asked seriously.

"If that's what you want."

"Then I'd have to say yes!"

"Well, that doesn't seem like much of a sacrifice," I said. I thought for a moment, and then my eyes caught her TV. It reminded me of the local news report on crop circles I'd seen the other day. "What if he lived on another planet?"

"Like an alien?" she asked, then grinned.

"Yes," I said. "Would you still go?"

Aunt Libby paused, really contemplating my question. I was growing weary as I waited for her answer.

"Is the planet environmentally sound?" she asked.

"This is a game, Aunt Libby!"

"I want to give truthful answers."

"The planet is environmentally sound and it is illegal to eat meat."

"Then I'd have to say, 'I'm there.'"

"Now," I said, building up steam to my point, "what if he was a vampire? Would you let him turn you?"

She paused. "Sure, why not?"

"That's it? No thoughts? No asking about the Underworld? You'd have to drink blood and sleep in a coffin."

"You told me not to analyze it. Besides, it's just a game, remember? Now your turn," she said, turning the tables on me. "How far would you go to prove your love to Alexander? Would you move?"

"Out of Dullsville? In a heartbeat. Besides, my mom wouldn't be able to nag me to clean up my room."

"Would you move to another planet for him?"

"Sure," I began. "Then I really wouldn't have to clean my room at all. My clothes would just float in space and I'd never have to pick them up."

We both cracked up.

Then my aunt became serious. "If he was a vampire—would you let him turn you?"

The truth was Alexander *was* a vampire. This question was the most difficult to answer because I thought about it every day. There was no doubt I wanted to be bonded to Alexander for all eternity. But did I want everything else that went with it? If Alexander already rejected the world I'd be entering, how would we live in it together?

"Well, would you?" my aunt pressed.

I placed my tea mug on the coffee table next to the burning incense. "This was supposed to be about you and Devon!" I said. I sat back, cross-legged. "Have you been to his house?"

"Not yet. He says he's not a good housekeeper."

Hmmm, I thought. *He could be covering up the fact he sleeps in a coffin.*

"Is he a carnivore?"

"I just remembered—" She got up and returned with her hobo-style purse and fished inside it. "You'd asked if I had a picture of Devon," she said, pulling out a digital camera.

She fiddled with a few buttons on the back. "I took this today," she said, and showed me the picture display. It was a picture of Devon, handsomely grinning, outside the blown-glass figurine booth. "I would have taken more, but he hates to have his picture taken."

I was surprised. I'd been so totally caught up in proving that Devon was a vampire, I'd stopped leaving room for any other conclusion.

"Here you are in the background," she said, pointing. I appeared to be talking to myself. "Funny, Alexander got cut off. He was standing right next to you."

Aunt Libby blew out all the candles, gave me a good-night squeeze, and headed off for bed.

Now that it was confirmed Devon was a normal mortal, I'd be able to sleep soundly, knowing the worst fate my aunt could suffer was a broken heart.

11

The Crop Circle

The following day Aunt Libby insisted I keep my evening date with Alexander, not only because "he is so handsome," as she put it, but because she was overdue for a yoga workout. While my aunt was going to stretch her body and mind, I was going to spend the evening glued to Alexander. But I still had ages before sunset and I could either hang out in Aunt Libby's apartment or go to Hipsterville's library. I chose neither and opted for a little adventure.

A few miles across town lay a mysterious crop circle that needed to be investigated. Phoenix would be confronting Jagger there at sunset and I might get a hint of their conversation and be back in time for Alexander's and my date.

At the very least, I was intrigued by the crop circles

and had to know who or what was making them. Were they really signals for vampires? Why did Jagger have all the hoax material stashed in his apartment? I wondered what the circle looked like up close.

According to the directions I got online, the same number seven bus that had previously taken me to the manor house made its way even farther through town and stopped a mile away from Mr. Sears's farm.

The RBI—Raven Bureau of Investigation—was back in business and on the hunt. Just in case of dangerous situations before me, I geared up with garlic powder, mace, and a flashlight borrowed from underneath Aunt Libby's sink.

Dullsville had its share of graffiti, vandals, and trespassers but nothing as exciting as an all-out alien invasion. Besides, if aliens traveled a million light-years to earth, I'm sure they'd be bummed to find they'd arrived in the boring town of Dullsville, U.S.A. Hipsterville, on the other hand, might make a great pit stop on the way to New York or Paris.

But if my presumption was right and the boy on TV had seen hovering bats, the guy at the Dungeon bar was speaking fact, and Jagger's mess was actually clues, the crop circles had the markings of a vampire.

Perhaps the farmer was selling tickets to his nine-acre backyard. I half expected the number seven to be transformed into a tour bus. But there was nothing unusual about the number seven or its riders, and when the bus lurched at the stop, I was the only one who disembarked.

The directions I had were pointing me to a single dirt road that separated luscious trees on one side from acres of wheat on the other.

I was in the middle of nowhere and the sun was already beginning to set over the farmhouse. When I explored the Mansion or the manor house, there were at least other houses within the sound of a scream.

I was exhilarated as I was terrified as I hurried along the lonely dirt road.

This was a prime spot for an alien or vampire sighting. There was nothing around for miles.

All at once, I felt someone or something behind me. I held on to the flashlight with one hand and the mace with the other, the garlic powder inches away in my purse. I was confident I could talk myself out of a situation if I was confronted by the farmer or one of his neighbors, but I could see the latter was a remote possibility.

Maybe I was imagining things. After all, I'd grown up watching *Children of the Corn* and *The Texas Chainsaw Massacre*.

Farmer Sears seemed jovial on TV, though. Either way, I still was primed for a unique encounter and hummed to myself softly to keep calm.

A dog barked in the distance, and I saw a small girl run out from the farmhouse and bring the animal inside.

There was only a fence that surrounded the house and another one that ran alongside the wheat field. Perhaps that's why it was so easy for some kids to pull a midnight prank.

I decided to stay clear of the farmhouse so Farmer Sears wouldn't come out "a-shootin'." A few minutes later, I was far enough away to climb over the fence and bury myself in the rows of wheat. The surroundings were actually quite beautiful. There were no city or town lights, and the stars were so visible and vibrant I wasn't sure they were real.

I was heading through the stalks when I saw what I thought to be crows flying over a scarecrow posted a few yards ahead. As I approached the raggedy stuffed man, I realized that the flying creatures were bats. I crept closer until they vanished.

It was then that I noticed that a few more yards ahead of me, in the middle of the wheat field, a circle as large as my house was mashed into the ground.

The circle was even more thrilling than when I'd seen it on TV. It was hard to make out its gigantic circumference, but it must have been the size of a spaceship. I couldn't imagine Jagger actually doing this alone. For a moment I wondered if in fact it was made by something other than vampires or human life.

I was actually surprised when I remembered the farmer's curious reaction on TV. I would have been furious. Whoever or whatever had destroyed a lot of his wheat.

I followed the circle for quite some time, scanning and

probing the dirt for anything unusual. I wasn't a scientist from NASA, but I could tell that there weren't any rocks or life-forms that I hadn't seen before.

It was getting harder to inspect in the dark, so I had decided to turn on my flashlight when I heard voices coming from the opposite side of the field. I was sure Farmer Sears had spotted me nosing around. I switched off my light, doubled back, and raced into the rows of stalks.

I was ready to hightail it out of there and call off my crop circle adventure when I glanced back to see the farmer. I caught a glimpse of white hair. I immediately ducked and poked my head between the stalks.

Jagger and two burly guys with tattoos and dressed in camouflage were examining the circle.

I didn't move.

"There's been TV coverage," Jagger said. "It's been all over the news. This is good."

"I thought you wanted the club to be a secret," the taller member of his crew said.

"From mortals, stupid. Not us. That's why we're out here making sure these stay intact," Jagger said, surveying the smashed wheat. "Vampires have been using crop circles for centuries to signal other vampires about areas where there's an Underworld presence. But mortals can't fathom our genius, so instead they think these are being made by extraterrestrials. It's really best for both worlds."

"But we are attracting others that can make trouble for us," the shaved-headed one confessed, following behind.

"No one can make trouble while I'm in charge," Jagger argued.

"There are others who don't want to follow your plan," said his burly cohort. "Not everyone wants you to be in charge, Jagger."

Shocked, Jagger spun back and confronted his bald supporter. "Excuse me?"

"It's true," the taller one said, defending his friend. "We've heard rumors. There are others who think the club should remain as just a club. Nothing more. We just wanted you to know."

"Anyone who dares to undermine me will have to deal with not only me but a gang of bloodthirsty vampires."

Just then I saw a purple head rise behind Jagger and his cohorts. They were startled as much as I was.

"I didn't hear your bike," Jagger said, bewildered.

"What are you guys doing out here?" Phoenix asked.

"I should be asking you that. We are expanding our club—my club. And maybe it's time we revoke your membership."

"You can't. Can you?" Phoenix challenged. "I have eternal membership. I thought that's what you wanted when you started the Dungeon."

"I did, but on my terms. Now out of our way; we have work to do."

Phoenix stepped before him. "We don't need more

members," Phoenix argued. "It's time you and your crew stop making these circles. There are plenty of our kind already in town. If we continue increasing our size, we increase our chance—"

"Of infiltrating the town?" Jagger asked with a sinister smile.

"Of being run out of town," Phoenix said firmly.

"You don't care about the club's direction. All you care about is seizing control of it. And then who knows what you'll do with it?"

"It's time for a new leader when the old one has undermined his followers. You're inviting vampires to this town for the sole purpose of taking it over."

"It's time to be part of the town. I'm tired of hiding. Now that I have a strong membership, we'll be able to roam freely amongst the mortals. We have a right to be known, and that decision is not yours to make."

"Nor is it yours," Phoenix said, his arms crossed. "You created a great club—a place for vampires to hang out in secret and be ourselves, without a threat to them or us. Where both worlds could live peacefully. But you let your ego get in the way. And now you are planning on destroying the very thing you created."

"I'm planning on expanding it."

"Not while I'm around."

"Don't you realize that you are outnumbered? And that when we get more members, you won't stand a chance?"

Jagger's gang surrounded him.

"No one appointed you," Phoenix challenged. "I will take you down."

"Then why don't you do it here? Now?"

Jagger's thugs closed their circle.

"It's too easy," Phoenix said defiantly. "I want to do it where everyone can see you fail."

There was something so fiery and powerful about Phoenix. Though he stood alone before Jagger and the other two muscle-bound vampires, he was still not threatened.

They closed in tighter.

"Don't even think about it," Phoenix said, undeterred. "Or we'll end this whole matter right here."

Jagger was quiet for a moment—then called off his gang. "This won't be the last of me. You can talk big here, in the middle of a field, but I have the club behind me."

With that, Jagger and his thugs disappeared into the darkness.

Phoenix remained in place. I could barely breathe. If he didn't even flinch in the company of three frightening vampires, what was a mere mortal like me to do?

He walked up to the stalks—only a few feet away from where I was hiding.

I didn't move a muscle or exhale.

I closed my eyes. At any moment he was going to find me. I finally opened my eyes. Phoenix was nowhere in sight. He had vanished.

I waited for a moment, making sure the coast was

clear. I raced back through the field, over the fence, and up the lonely dirt road. I waved my arms and shouted frantically as a number seven retreated up the adjacent road. A passenger saw me and signaled the driver.

As the bus pulled away and I slumped down in an empty seat in the back, I heard the sound of a motorcycle passing and racing off down the road.

12

A Date with a Vampire

I hopped off the number seven at Aunt Libby's stop, wiped my soiled boots, and removed the untwined pieces of wheat tangled in my hair and clothes. I played over the crop circle encounter in my mind. I couldn't believe I'd been so wrong about Phoenix—I had only imagined the purple-haired biker who seemed far more mysterious and brooding to be even more dangerous than Alexander's nemesis. Underneath all his bravado, he wanted the club to remain secret, and when he had found out there were other plans for it, he began a plan of his own. I had misjudged Phoenix, like students at Dullsville High had always misjudged me.

It seemed like an eternity before I spotted the black Mercedes driving down the tree-lined street. Alexander opened the car door for me and I ran to his side. After a quick smooch and a honk from a minivan waiting behind us, I climbed into the car and we drove off.

"Where are you taking me?" I asked as we headed through downtown and up a long and winding hill.

"We haven't been able to spend time exploring town, so I thought I'd take you to a place where we could," said Alexander.

Alexander continued to motor up the winding road, which was so steep at times that it seemed as if we were driving at a right angle. At the top of the hill sat a bell tower that pointed to the heavens. He turned into the cracked black-topped lot, avoiding several potholes, and parked.

"This is the bell tower I saw when Aunt Libby and I were waiting for you at the art festival!"

The white-painted bell tower was a historic landmark dating back to the 1800s. It was simple in its design with an observation deck and working clock. The paint was chipping and the roof was in disrepair. An oversized sign, placed by an old well a few yards away, apologized to visitors for the inconvenience of the ongoing renovation.

Alexander and I crept on the cracked sidewalk, stepping over plastic sheets and discarded nails. A stick, wedged in the front door, kept it slightly ajar.

Back in Alexander's company, the Underworld, Dullsville, and the Dungeon were distant memories.

Once inside, we climbed three flights of stairs that led to the bell tower door. I held on to Alexander's hand and followed him through the door and up a seemingly never-ending spiral staircase. When we finally ascended to the top, we were so high above the town, I thought I could reach out and touch the stars.

An enormous copper bell hung from a cast-iron A-frame beam. I touched the rusty bell, which was weathered and tarnished. There wasn't a cord or a hired bell ringer in sight. The bell must have weighed a quarter ton, and even if I worked out regularly, I wouldn't be able to make it ring.

"What if the bell automatically chimes?" I asked Alexander. "It'll be deafening."

"Not this antique," he said, tapping his hand against it. "It hasn't rung in years. Look." He showed me a bird's nest and cobwebs in the cast-iron tresses.

Alexander directed me around the bell. Awaiting us was a lit candelabra, votives, a black lace tablecloth set before the archway. His backpack looked full of goodies.

"This is beautiful!" I hugged him with all my might. I held Alexander's hand as an anchor as I inched a safe distance to the archway and peered out. I'd spent several nights buried underneath the lowest depths of Hipsterville. This night I'd spend the evening at its highest point.

It was breathtaking. The yellow stars filled the night sky and twinkled as if they were winking at us. We had a panoramic view of Hipsterville. The town looked like a miniature layout found in a retail display window—the kind with tiny lights, trees, and cars.

I leaned against Alexander, my arm wrapped around his waist and his around my shoulder, as we gazed out into the picturesque evening.

"I think I see Aunt Libby's apartment," I said, pointing to a group of town houses.

"I think I can see into her window," he said, teasing me. "Even I don't have that kind of vision."

"Well . . . I think that's her apartment."

"But your aunt Libby lives in that part of town," he said, nodding toward an area of homes a few miles over.

I had no sense of direction.

"Well, I know over there is Main Street. And there's a park, the train station, and the art museum," I said, proudly gesturing to obvious places of interest.

"Did I tell you you are the most beautiful tour guide I've ever seen?" He picked me up and spun me around and gave me a passionate kiss. When he set me down, not only did the bell tower spin, but so did the town.

I latched on to him until I was steady.

"I wanted to bring you to a place where we could explore all of the town together in one evening," Alexander remarked.

"This is perfect!" I agreed.

We unpacked our dinner, specially prepared by Jameson. Alexander tore into his grilled steak sandwich and gulped down his red drink while I broke off pieces of French bread. I was so distracted by the beautiful night, fresh air, and my handsome boyfriend that I had little appetite.

I marveled at how much Alexander enjoyed his food.

"Maybe I'll cook for you someday," I offered.

"Really? You know how?"

"I'm great at mac and cheese and steak fries. Or I can prepare a mean bowl of cereal."

Alexander beamed. "I may have to take you up on that."

Then I rested my head against his lap as he sipped his bottle of thick liquid.

When we'd finished and cleaned up, we leaned against an archway, a safe distance from the ledge but in full view of the town. I sat back, entranced, watching Alexander against the sparkling lights of Hipsterville.

Each time Alexander took me on a date, it was more spectacular than the one before. He spent as much time thinking about and preparing for our dates as he did creating one of his paintings. My heart would skyrocket with the touch of his hand, or an unearthly kiss. At the same time, I was comforted knowing there was no place on earth I'd rather be than by his side.

"I have something for you," he said, digging into the backpack.

I imagined him presenting me with a small jewelry box—perhaps a ring—or a larger gift, such as a bouquet of dead black roses.

Instead he handed me a flat package, the size of an envelope, neatly wrapped in black lace.

I tore the fabric off the package in wild anticipation of its contents. It was a one-way bus ticket to Dullsville.

"Aren't you excited?" he asked, beaming as bright as the stars above us.

"Sure . . ."

He seemed disappointed with my reaction. "I thought

it was what you wanted. Jameson and I have already begun packing."

"It is . . . But you're still here. Aunt Libby. And the—"

"The what?"

"Uh . . . the . . . summer. Freedom."

"We'll spend summer at home. Together."

"You're right. It's the best gift ever," I said, giving him a kiss.

When I was finally delivered the news I'd been waiting to hear since Alexander left Dullsville, I wasn't as pleased as I'd imagined. Alexander couldn't return to Dullsville now, when the Dungeon was on the brink of upheaval. I'd just begun hanging out with Aunt Libby, and I longed to dance and gossip until dawn with Scarlet and Onyx. And I was desperate to know what was going to happen to Jagger and Phoenix. I wasn't ready for it to end.

Alexander was set on leaving. There wasn't any way for me to stall the departure. Or perhaps there might be one way . . . I'd have to play the Coffin Club card.

If I told Alexander about the Dungeon, he'd be forced to have me show him and delay our departure. I was assured of at least a few more days, or rather nights, of us inspecting the underground club. Maybe it was time I told him everything.

"I've heard that Devon was right," I suddenly said. "There is a vampire club here!"

"It's just a rumor. You believe gossip?" he challenged.

"What if it is true? Don't you think we should stay and check it out?"

Alexander placed his hand on mine. "Our trip here is over. We both got what we came for. Valentine is out of Dullsville and safely back in Romania. And you and I are together."

"But—"

"Let's enjoy our last evening here," he said. He made sure we did, too, by placing his pink lips on my black ones.

When Alexander playfully nibbled on my neck, it made me think of one more thing.

I pulled back.

"What's wrong?"

I paused. The night, the view, and Alexander were all gorgeous. I was in the arms of a very real vampire—one whom I loved and who loved me back. I'd also spent several days surrounded by other vampires. I'd met new friends, like Onyx and Scarlet, and was given a glimpse of their world. It wasn't ghastly or deadly after all. I wondered if several days were in fact enough for me when I could be living in it for eternity.

And if I were to be turned, what a romantic time and place to have it done. But really . . . was I ready?

"Nothing's wrong," I finally answered. "I was just wondering."

"About what?"

"About me . . . becoming like you."

He pulled back and appeared cross.

"I'm just saying. You're here, I'm here, the moon is full."

"Really. It's that easy for you?" he pressed skeptically.

"I think you think I won't be able to handle it."

"You have a romantic view of my world. Probably like I do of yours."

"But I know more about your world than you think."

"I'm not your typical vampire. . . ."

"You're not typical in any way. You are one of a kind. It's just that . . . I want you to consider me as part of your world."

"I do already. From the moment I met you."

Alexander was dreamy, his face framed against the sparkling moonlight.

He was right. I was so concerned with living in another world, I wasn't appreciating the one we were in together.

I smiled and fell into his arms.

"When you turn me," I began, "will we have a covenant ceremony? Will we invite friends? Or will you just hold me, on a perfect night like this?"

"Well. All I need to do is start here." He took my fingers and kissed them, then worked his way up my hand and forearm. My flesh tingled as he continued to kiss up my arm and the nape of my neck. "Then lean in . . ."

Suddenly Alexander's eyes turned red and he looked away. "It's time to go," he said.

"Already? But we just got here."

"We've been here for hours. It's getting late," he said.

"I didn't mean to—"

But Alexander had already slung his backpack over his shoulder and taken my hand. "I have a lot to do before I leave."

"Can I help you pack?" I asked, standing on my tiptoes like a child.

"That won't be necessary. Jameson is very organized."

I wasn't ready for us to separate and there was nothing I could say to change his mind. Before I knew it we were standing outside Aunt Libby's apartment.

"So when I see you next," Alexander began, "you'll be outside the Mansion's gates, just like the painting."

"I will."

Alexander kissed me long. "I'm glad you came to visit me."

It felt like I needed a crowbar to pry me away. My heart began to sink as he let me go.

I held the bus ticket in my hand. I'd gotten everything I'd come for—to reunite with Alexander and to finally know he was returning to Dullsville.

"Thank you again for my present," I said.

Alexander waited for me to safely enter my aunt's apartment. Once inside, I attempted to replace the key ring in my purse. Something sparkled—a long, old-fashioned, golden key. It was the Dungeon skeleton key.

The whole time Alexander had been in Hipsterville, he had been painting a picture of me outside the Mansion. During our separation, he'd been thinking about me living in Dullsville as much as I'd been dreaming about him on my trip.

And now, as I held the skeleton key in my hand, I was thinking about one more place—an empty tomb overtaken by dancing vampires deep below Hipsterville's new club.

Alexander was right. It was time to leave Hipsterville. But if, in fact, I'd be boarding a Dullsville-bound bus without promise of seeing or visiting a true vampire club again, I had to see the Dungeon one last time.

13

The Dungeon

Aunt Libby's fifteen-year-old navy blue Schwinn was no sexy Harley Night Rod. The tires were low on air, the handlebar was missing a rubber handle cover, and the back wheel squeaked with every revolution.

I peddled through Hipsterville and coasted down Main Street, steering around discarded trash left over from the festival. I locked the Schwinn to a bicycle rack outside the library, a block south of the vampire club.

I was hoofing down the sidewalk when I heard a motorcycle whizzing through an alleyway. I followed the sound, which seemed to be coming from behind the buildings. I wandered off the beaten path to a lit alleyway outside the Coffin Club, where I spotted a hearse parked next to a Dumpster. The car was familiar—a vintage black Cadillac with a silver bat hood ornament, whitewall tires, skull and crossbones on the left rear panel, and a skeleton hanging on the rearview mirror. The license plate's county sticker was from Hipsterville and the license plate read: I BITE. It was Jagger's.

Past the oversized garbage can, I glimpsed a rider with a black helmet parking his bike in the alley. I crept over as silently and quickly as a daddy longlegs. When the rider took off his helmet, he spun around. The shadows blocked him, but I appeared in full view.

Even in the shadows, I could tell he seemed surprised by my arrival.

Phoenix headed toward me, gravely concerned. "There may be trouble inside the bar tonight," he warned.

"Trouble? That's my middle name."

"I'm serious." He placed his hand firmly on my shoulder. "I strongly suggest you go home."

He glared down at me, brooding behind his sunglasses, his dark purple and black hair flopping seductively over them.

I had a feeling that if I stayed, there might be more trouble outside the club.

I nodded reluctantly.

Phoenix slipped into the Coffin Club through the back alley entrance. I was surprised he hadn't parked in the VIP spot and sauntered into the club like a leather-clad prince. Maybe there was going to be a fight inside the club tonight and he wanted to make a quick getaway. I lagged behind him, and as the door began to close I stuck my foot inside the frame. The door was heavy as it slammed on my boot. I limped inside.

I saw purple locks bobbing a few feet ahead of me before they disappeared through a door. I hobbled into the darkness, doing my best to keep up, but kept a safe distance so I would go undetected. All of a sudden I was descending a steep staircase and standing in front of a dungeon door with the spray-painted words DEAD END.

I uncovered my Coffin Club bracelet, poked in my purse for my key chain, and anxiously fumbled for the skeleton key. An equal amount of fear and excitement coursed through my veins. The key shook in my unsteady hand, but I managed after a few tries to stick it into the lock and swiftly turn it.

The door creaked open.

Dragon examined me as I whisked past him and slipped through the slit in the curtain.

The Dungeon was spectacularly alive. Clubsters were buzzing, dancing, tipping back goblets, and partying as if it might be their final time at the club. The devilish and decadent catacomb chambers were packed full of fang-toothed goths, punks, and emos. Perhaps it would be the last time I'd see Scarlet and Onyx, if they forgave me for recognizing them as they were going unnoticed in the mortal world.

But as I milled through the crowd, an even darker mood began to wash over the club like draining blood. I spotted members in white T-shirts with the black word POSSESS, in homage to Jagger's tattoo, having private meetings, whispering, and passing messages.

"Raven!" I heard a familiar girl's voice call. It was

Onyx. Her hair was styled in long pigtails, with spiderweb bows. She and Scarlet raced over to me.

"I'm so sorry we pretended not to know you at the art festival," Scarlet apologized.

"Will you ever forgive us?" Onyx asked.

"We have to keep a low profile when we're in the mortal world," said Scarlet.

"Me too, but sometimes I forget," I said.

"I couldn't acknowledge that we'd met here," said Onyx.

"I understand," I replied. "What was I thinking?"

But I did feel sad. As much as I didn't fit in Dullsville, I was still me—24-7. I didn't really know what it meant to hide part of me—or all of me—from others, like Onyx, Scarlet, Jagger, and Alexander did on a daily basis. While Alexander thrived on isolation and Jagger on his menacing ego, they all were truly outsiders. I realized more than ever that for many of the vampires like Scarlet and Onyx, this club was their only lifeline.

"There is so much going on," Scarlet said, her voice rife with concern.

"Can't you feel the tension?" Onyx asked. "The club's about to explode!"

"I know—there's something I've got to tell you . . ." I began.

"Something's going down tonight," Scarlet interrupted.

"It's going to be a late night tonight, if you need to crash here," Onyx offered.

"You sleep in the club?" I wondered aloud.

"Scar doesn't," Onyx began. "She lives in town. But I hang here when I visit. That's what's so cool about the club and why we're hoping it doesn't change.

"Would you like to see my crash pad?" Onyx asked proudly. "We can tell you more there—"

"Yes," I declared enthusiastically.

I was curious to see what kind of sleeping chamber Jagger had set up for the club members to entice them to Hipsterville.

Once again, I was guided through narrow winding catacombs, past chambers, hallowed graves, and tombs. Everything looked familiar, and at the same time I knew I'd never been down these tunnels before. We finally stopped in front of a gray metal sliding door. Onyx opened the portal. Never in my life had I imagined such a vampire dwelling.

The windowless room was the size of a warehouse. It was a funeral director's dream come true. One coffin after another lay on the dirt floor, perfectly lined up—ten coffins across. But what was even more macabre were the coffins suspended above them, hanging from the ceiling by steel wire, like cryptic hammocks.

With a slam, the portal closed behind us.

I waited for the coffin lids to pop open and fang-flashing vampires to yell, "Surprise!" But nothing happened. I must have appeared unusually pale because Scarlet placed her bloodred-fingernailed hand on my shoulder. "Don't be startled," she reassured me. "It's just a fire door."

"Let me show you my coffin," Onyx said excitedly.

I wasn't sure how their owners could tell them apart because they all appeared identical. We walked by the vampires' beds to the front of the room.

"This one is mine," she said, tapping on the top.

On one side was a black onyx stone, outlined in white. She lifted the coffin lid. Inside were red and black plaid sheets, a comforter and matching pillowcase, a black iPod, and a black UglyDoll Ice Bat.

She closed the lid casually, as if it were a life-size guitar case.

When I'd pictured becoming a vampire, I'd never imagined this—sleeping among strangers like in a youth hostel for the undead, just for the chance to wake up, dance, and be with other vampires. Was this the life I'd be leading if I joined the Underworld? To remain forever in a hidden identity—or to risk it all to be known around mortals?

It was time I told Onyx and Scarlet about the crop circle and what I'd overheard.

"We were wrong—I was wrong. About Phoenix. He doesn't want to expose the club. He wants us to remain peaceful."

"You're kidding," Onyx said in disbelief.

Scarlet's eyes grew red with rage. "Then it's just been Jagger . . . all along."

"Yes! He and Phoenix confronted each other out by the crop circle. Jagger's been inviting vampires here under the guise of a safe club to hang out in, but all the time he was planning on gathering enough members to take over the town."

"He duped us all along!" Scarlet exclaimed.

"We must do something before he ruins the club—and us!" Onyx ordered.

The portal opened. It was Scarlet's blond date and he appeared very concerned. "There you are!" He charged over to Scarlet. "Something's going down . . ." He paused when he saw me. "I'm afraid we are going to lose the club."

Before he had a chance to explain, he grabbed Scarlet's hand, who in turn took Onyx's. Onyx grasped mine, her soft palm perspiring. I grew even more anxious—what would make a vampiress nervous?

We entered the labyrinth of dark and narrow catacombs. It was like a Halloween haunted house, only the costumed volunteers were real-life vampires. Fanged, corpse-complexioned, blue-lipped vampires, all wearing white T-shirts, hung from the archways as we hurried through. They threatened us, licking lips, eyes red with anger, reaching for us and trying to take hold of anything, from our shirts to our skirts. Parts of the catacombs were so curvy I was afraid we'd get separated. Other turns were so dark the only thing I felt was Onyx's hand and my boots hitting the uneven dirt floor.

When a naked bulb eventually illuminated our path, I was sure it wasn't Onyx's hand I was holding anymore. When I looked up, I let out a horrible scream. A red-eyed vampire was clutching my hand, his nails as long as knives. Before I could give him a quick karate chop or stomp on his checkered Vans, Onyx got in his face, her eyes bright with fury, and yanked me away from him.

Someone jumped out of the shadows, blocking my way. "Vote for Jagger if you know what's good for you."

I had managed to leap around him when another vampire, looking down from an archway, warned, "Jagger has the only bloodline worth following."

Onyx squeezed my hand and I received a tremendous tug, hurling me and our chain forward. We all spilled out and landed safely in a chamber where mystical fog permeated the air and a line of members waited, their destination unclear. We'd made it out of the catacombs.

In the chamber stood podiums cornered off by a red velvet curtain. One by one, members entered the booths as if they were voting in a national election.

"Sign in," a vampire ordered, directing us to a sheet of butcher paper scrolled on a long oak table.

Onyx picked up a feather dipped in ink and wrote her name, as beautiful as calligraphy. I scribbled down *Raven Madison*.

"What are we voting for?" I asked Onyx.

"The direction of the club."

The guy handed us a piece of weathered parchment paper the size of a paperback, a pin encased in a plastic container, and an alcohol swab.

"Where's the pen?" I asked.

"This is it," he said disdainfully, rattling the container encasing the pin.

"I'm not really sure—" I began as another member

routed me to a stall just behind Onyx's.

He closed the red velvet curtain around me. I placed my parchment on the podium. Two vampire names faced me—JAGGER and PHOENIX—an empty box next to each. Underneath Jagger's name appeared EXPAND DUNGEON. Underneath Phoenix's were the words LOCK DUNGEON.

I waited a moment for instructions, but none came. Unlike school, there were no teachers or printed directions, e.g., "Completely fill in the circle," "Use a number two pencil," or "Press firmly."

I was in a vampire club, after all—there could be only one way to vote.

I sterilized my finger with a wipe, then took a deep breath and pricked my skin. I was so nervous, I figured I'd bleed to death, but instead not even a drop surfaced. With my other hand, I squeezed my finger with all my might. A drop of blood the size of a dot formed, then it grew as big as a pencil's eraser. As if my finger were a pen, I marked a box with a bloody **X**.

I caught up to Onyx, Scarlet, and their deadly dates by the electric chair. We wasted no time in returning to the dance floor, now infused with worried clubsters. There was less dancing and more talking, huddling, and pacing. The stage was empty of bandmates or instruments.

I wasn't sure what we were waiting for exactly—a celebration? A fight? After all, I was in a vampire club—we could be waiting for a sacrifice.

A few minutes later, Dragon took the stage holding a stack of parchment ballots. He awkwardly stepped to the microphone. He obviously appeared more comfortable confronting members by the coffin lid door than he did speaking in front of them.

He shifted back and forth uneasily and cleared his throat. "The results are in," he declared, one hand in his camouflage cargo pocket.

The crowd burst into cheers. White-T-shirt-wearing members chanted, "Jagger, Jagger" while others shouted, "Phoenix, Phoenix."

Phoenix and Jagger, flanked with their cohorts, entered the stage from opposite sides like prizefighters coming into a ring.

Jagger threw his arms up in the air while Phoenix folded his arms and hung back.

Dragon cleared his throat again. "And now . . . what you've all waited for. . . . The Dungeon master is . . ."

Everyone fell silent.

Then Dragon leaned into the microphone and yelled, "The Dungeon master is . . . Phoenix!"

The crowd cheered, although the members in white T-shirts were visibly disappointed.

I grabbed Scarlet's hand. The girls wailed in delight and we raised our arms and danced.

Dragon stood twice as tall and three times as wide as Jagger.

"It is time, Jagger, that you relinquish your Master Key," he demanded, and took the lanyard from around Jagger's neck.

Dragon returned to the mike. "This is one of a kind

and can't be duplicated," Dragon announced. "It is the only key that can permanently lock or unlock the club, giving the holder total control."

Phoenix took to the microphone to thunderous applause and cheers while Dragon presented him with a shiny golden skeleton key.

The crowd cheered again as Phoenix nodded his acceptance. "For our own survival," he began in his heavy Romanian accent, "we must remain peaceful and anonymous. The Dungeon has become a perfect place for us to be ourselves. We don't have to be violent to be vampires."

The crowd cheered with enthusiasm.

"And what is most important is that we don't look to one person as a leader. So as long as we remain on a peaceful path, I relinquish control to the real leaders of the club—you!"

Phoenix high-fived his gang and stepped offstage and disappeared.

"This is awesome!" Scarlet yelled.

Onyx and Scarlet clasped hands with me and we jumped up and down, giggling and cheering like a daisy circle. Onyx's pigtails and Scarlet's curls bounced like those of girls in a school yard.

Jagger hopped onstage and seized the microphone. "Don't be so ready to turn your club over to him!" The noise died down and finally stopped. Everyone was confused by Jagger's reappearance.

"One of our members is a fraud!" he challenged. "In

fact, she isn't a member at all! We are a club of immortals and one of us is actually a mortal!"

Whispers quickly spread throughout the club like wild-fire. I was honestly so caught up in the moment, I gasped along with Scarlet and Onyx.

"The voting result is null and void!" Jagger argued. "Phoenix is not your winner!"

"That's weird," Onyx remarked to me. "Who would want to be a mortal surrounded by vampires? Do they have a death wish?"

"I demand a recount!" Jagger yelled.

Jagger's gang stood onstage and examined the stack of ballots one by one.

The crowd was on edge as if they were waiting for an execution order.

Several of Phoenix's supporters climbed onstage and surrounded Jagger's crew.

"One of these is not true vampire blood," Jagger said, waving the stack in the air.

"Here it is!" one of Jagger's sidekicks hollered like he'd found a winning lottery ticket.

Jagger snatched it from his hand.

"This one is mortal blood!" he proclaimed. "I told you! Taste it for yourself!"

The confused group of immortals was now talking quietly among themselves.

"I know who the mortal is!" Jagger declared.

The crowd began to skeptically glance around. No one

believed the person beside them might not be one of the undead. For a moment I didn't either. Perhaps it was someone else he was talking about.

The ghastly group looked to Jagger for an answer.

Jagger was fuming with anger. "The mortal is hiding among you. And she's standing right there!" he blurted out, pointing to me.

The clubsters gasped in disbelief.

My stomach caved in. At any moment the crowd of vampires was going to pounce on me.

Dragon pushed his way to the microphone. "It doesn't matter!" he said, holding my ballot and the focus of the group. "Phoenix has twice as many votes as you."

His already ghost white face turned paler.

"Phoenix won fair and square!" Dragon proclaimed.

The crowd cheered a deafening roar.

Jagger glared at them, then at me, his blue and green eyes turning fiery red. He threw the card down and stormed offstage.

One of his crew came to the microphone. "We still have a mortal among us!"

"Calm down," Dragon said, but the white-T-shirt-wearing members grew restless.

The whole crowd turned their gaze to me, baring their fangs.

"Remember why you voted for Phoenix," Dragon directed.

Scarlet and Onyx appeared bewildered.

"I'm so—," I pleaded.

"I thought you were our friend," Scarlet said, disappointed.

"I was. I am. Just because I'm mortal doesn't mean—"

Jagger's crew was closing in around us.

"You lied to us," Scarlet argued.

"Did I? I never said I was a vampire."

"She's right," Onyx defended. "We liked her because she's cool. And that hasn't changed. In fact, she's brave. I never would have hung out with vampires before I was turned."

"I didn't mean to—," I said to Scarlet.

Then Scarlet's demeanor softened. "It doesn't matter to me that you are mortal," she agreed. "I liked you because you are you."

The rest of the club was far less forgiving. Jagger's crew encircled me.

"She may reveal everything to the outside world," one said.

"And destroy our anonymity!" cried another.

"She needs to make a decision!"

"You better turn now!" one demanded.

"You must decide for all eternity," one said seductively. "You won't regret it."

"There is only one way to be a member!" another ordered, his gold fangs flashing.

"Our way is the best way," someone added.

"We are offering you the chance for immortality. Would you rather be buried in a grave or just sleep in one?"

"Come join us. We won't bite . . ." one said with a laugh.

Scarlet linked tightly on to one of my arms and Onyx the other.

"Back off!" Onyx yelled.

The two girls held on to me like a prized possession, but I felt more like a piñata. They were no match for the angry mob of Jagger's crew, and it took only a few moments before our hold was broken.

I stood alone, surrounded by bloodthirsty vampires. The rest of the club was motionless. Even Phoenix's benign vampires, who wanted nothing more than a secure place to hang out, were now conflicted. Was I more of a threat alive—or undead?

I'd always fantasized about becoming a vampire, hanging limp-bodied in the arms of a seductive vampire lover. I'd be the only one who could sustain his eternal life. Without me, he wouldn't exist and he'd be buried deep within his coffin even in the moonlit hours. We'd live out our Underwordly lives together—shrouded in mystery. This is the picture I'd always had in my mind, and when I met Alexander, I felt this undying love for him—my dream was coming true.

But being seduced by a gang of Jagger's cohorts wasn't what I'd imagined. I was living the nightmare I'd had a few nights ago. I wasn't ready to give up my mortal life because of peer pressure. I'd waited forever for Alexander to be the one to turn me—not a gang of Underworldly strangers. I'd always wanted to become a vampire, but under the moonlight during a covenant ceremony, not in a club brawl. My heart raced. I hoped to wake up at any moment, out of breath on Aunt Libby's futon. It didn't happen.

"Don't touch her!" Onyx yelled as a few evil-looking vampires held her back.

"So you've been hanging out here . . ." a white T-shirt member said, slithering up next to me. "Is it what you always dreamed of?"

Jagger's crew inched closer, hovering around me like a flock of vultures.

"Yes! Just not this way."

"There is only one way to become a member of our club," one said as they tightened their circle.

I turned to my new friends, Onyx and Scarlet. And to the whole club that I'd been accepted in and wanted to remain part of. Though I was attracted, mesmerized, and even seduced by the Dungeon, when faced with the decision, was I willing to give up my life to join? At what cost did I want to be a member of the real Coffin Club?

At any moment, like an action hero, I hoped Alexander would burst through the Dungeon door.

But Alexander was nowhere to be found. He and Jameson were naively packing while I was moments away from becoming a vampiress.

Even Dragon wasn't in plain view. I'd have to get myself out of this mess. Only I didn't know how. The entrance was locked, and there was no getting past the gang of "POSSESS-ed."

"I've always wanted to be like you. That's why I'm here. Why I snuck in!" I shouted. "Don't you see?"

"Then join us!" one said.

"You will be eternally grateful," another proclaimed. They stared at me with hypnotic eyes. I became dizzy and shifted my gaze away.

"Not now, not this way!" I cried.

Two clubsters in POSSESS white T-shirts grasped my wrists and brushed my hair away from my shoulder.

I was overpowered. I couldn't move. My heart was pounding so hard I thought it would explode at any moment. "It won't hurt," they said, licking their lips.

"Well, it might sting a bit," one said, and leaned into me.

"No! Not this way. I want Alexander!"

Suddenly the sound of a motorcycle's engine tearing through the catacombs was heard.

Phoenix peeled out of the tunnel and screeched to a halt at the edge of the dance floor. He vehemently revved his engine repeatedly.

Several members stepped back, uncertain of Phoenix's next move. But the crew continued to latch on to my wrists even tighter.

Phoenix revved his engine again. When Jagger's crew didn't flinch, he shook his head. He thrust the motorcycle in reverse and backed it up ever so slowly, inch by inch, never taking his eyes off of me. He backed up as far as the farthermost archway—about twenty yards away from us—and shifted back into drive. My heart was throbbing louder than the engine itself. When my captives didn't release me, Phoenix revved the engine a final time. He took off and headed straight for me.

I froze. Everything was happening in slow motion. Phoenix sped toward me, his engine roaring, dust spraying behind him. The crowd on the dance floor quickly dispersed. My heart must have stopped and I forgot to breathe. He continued to race right for me. I tried desperately to wriggle out of the gang's clutches, but I couldn't as the Night Rod approached. At any second I was going to have motorcycle tracks racing up my body. Phoenix was now only a few feet away and still I couldn't move. I closed my eyes and said a quick prayer. At the very last second, Jagger's crew released me from their clutches and scrambled to the sides. I let out a bloodcurdling scream as the motorcycle skidded to a dead stop a few inches from where I was standing.

It took a moment before I could inhale again. My body was limp and my legs like buttered noodles. Phoenix hopped off his bike and extended his hand to me, but I refused. I still didn't know who this guy was. Maybe Phoenix wanted me to be the Dungeon Mistress.

He didn't grab my hand or lean in to bite me. He actually looked quite surprised.

Dragon resurfaced and, along with a large group of club members, gathered Jagger's crew together and repossessed their club keys.

Scarlet and Onyx ran over to me. "It's okay. Phoenix saved you. He's restored order to our club."

The crowd began chanting, "Phoenix, Phoenix" as the

two girls helped me straddle the sleek bike.

"I still have the Master Key," Phoenix announced with a thumbs-up to the crowd.

Everyone cheered.

I looked out into the crowd of immortals. They, like me, just wanted a place to hang out and be the insiders for a change.

The music began to blast and many cheered, kissed, or started to dance.

Onyx gave me a tight squeeze and I hugged her back as hard as I could. "Come back, please," she said, flashing her onyx-jeweled fang. "You have a lifetime membership."

"Keep in touch," Scarlet said. "You have my number. Just remember to call after sunset. My—"

". . . parents hate to be woken up during the day," we said in unison. Then we both giggled wildly.

I glanced around the Dungeon—the dance floor, the bar full of blood drinks, the hollowed-out graves and tombs used for life as much as for death in my world. I'd never been in a truly Underworldly environment, and I didn't know when or if I'd ever be in one again. I'd been surrounded by cold-blooded vampires who, I learned, surprisingly, were warmhearted. I'd found the club of my dreams—the only one I'd ever really wanted to belong to. Phoenix handed me his helmet and I placed it on my head. I wrapped my arms around his studded leather jacket and smiled at Scarlet and Onyx, now in the company of their dates. The members retreated, rocked to the music, and waved.

Phoenix started the engine and I held on to him with all my might as he drove off through the labyrinth of dark, winding catacombs and out a secret exit.

Phoenix sat on his motorcycle as I unlocked Aunt Libby's bike outside the library. I sensed his gaze as I wrapped the heavy metal chain around the Schwinn's seat.

Phoenix was leaning back against his bike, his motorcycle boots crossed at the ankle and his black leather pants hugging him hard like cellophane. His leather jacket was open, revealing a black T-shirt, and his arms were folded. Purple hair flopped over black sunglasses, and the moonlight cast a shadow against his pale face. He was staring straight at me—just like he was when I'd seen him illuminated in the Dungeon.

I didn't know what to say. Phoenix had saved my life.

And I wasn't sure when I'd see him again, or if I'd ever.

"I can't thank you enough—," I said from a safe distance.

"Well, you can try," he said coyly.

I smiled and playfully rolled my eyes. "I told you, I have a boyfriend."

For some reason I sensed that it didn't matter to him whether I surrendered to his advances or not. I almost felt that he preferred I didn't. He appeared to be the kind of guy who was comfortable living in the shadows while the other guy got the girl.

"I was wrong about you," I confessed. "You were much more benevolent than I imagined. I'm sorry I misjudged you."

He nodded. "That's all right," he replied. "I misjudged you, too."

"Really?" I asked.

"Yes. You were much more trouble than I imagined."

We both laughed. I knew I should have felt happy that Phoenix had saved me, but instead I felt really sad knowing I might never see my new vampire friend again.

I had started to straddle Aunt Libby's bike when I quickly climbed off and leaned it against the rack. I raced over to Phoenix and wrapped my arms around him, giving him a long, tight squeeze. I must have surprised him, because he didn't hug me back. Then I felt his leather-clad arms around me. He hugged me, too, as if it were for the last time.

I hopped on Aunt Libby's bike and sped away, not once glancing back. When I passed Main Street and turned the corner, I heard the familiar roaring sound of a motorcycle racing off into the night.

14

As I pedaled back toward Aunt Libby's, I was overtaken by a flood of emotions. I'd come here to Hipsterville for one reason only—to reunite with my boyfriend. However, once I'd gotten my wish, I'd defied his one request—I had returned to the Coffin Club without him.

Not only did I discover an intoxicating and dangerous underground world of vampires in the Dungeon, I had been one bite away from belonging to the Underworld for eternity—all without my beloved Alexander.

After falling in love with Alexander, it wasn't just that I wanted to become a vampire—I wanted to become one together.

Yet I immersed myself in a world that my own boyfriend himself felt like an outsider in. Was that what Alexander wanted for me? Or for himself?

I coasted downhill and replayed the last week in my

head. I thought I was being investigative and mature when perhaps I was only being reckless.

And if Alexander ever found out about my Dungeon adventures, I wanted him to hear it from my own lips. I wanted him to know that if and when I became immortal, he'd be the one on the other side of my neck.

I felt as if I'd betrayed Alexander. I was ashamed and disappointed in myself. I had to confess to Alexander all that I'd done. I had to let him know I'd been so close to joining his world but that without him it meant nothing.

Alexander was right to buy me a ticket out of town. He always knew what was best for me, and I'd taken the wrong path. Instead of taking a turn to head to Aunt Libby's, I veered left toward Lennox Hill. It began to rain.

I sped through the growing puddles and steered through the long street to the cul-de-sac that the manor house sat on.

I pedaled up the driveway and leaned the Schwinn against a small gate. I ran along the uneven rock path and banged against the front door.

No one answered. I stood back. I didn't see anyone lurking in the main room or attic room windows. Lightning flashed as I ran alongside the house and around to the back door. I pounded my fists on the door, droplets of rainwater bouncing off.

I climbed on top of a discarded box and peeked in the kitchen window. There were no signs of dishes, plates, flowers, or anything resembling the living. The already empty-looking manor now appeared totally vacant.

Frustrated, I ran through the unkempt gardens infested with overgrown weeds. I tried to peer into Alexander's attic window, but from my vantage point I couldn't get a clear view.

One thing had changed. There was no curtain in the window.

My heart sank. I kicked the corner of the wooden bench.

I had one last shot. I hurried to the garage. The lock had been removed and the door was slightly ajar. When I opened the garage door I was shocked—the Mercedes was gone.

That meant one thing—Alexander and Jameson had already left the manor house.

I wouldn't be able to fall into Alexander's arms and tell him about my terrifying night or explain that I didn't want to become a member of the real Coffin Club without him.

For now, my confession would have to wait.

I unhinged the Dungeon skeleton key from my key ring and symbolically placed it on the floor of the garage.

A streak of lightning lit the sky and I saw something in the garage sparkle. I inched forward to examine it more closely as the thunder crashed around me. I caught a glimpse of something behind a hanging sheet hidden in the shadows. Perhaps it was a coffin or mirrors from the manor house. Protruding from the sheet and catching the moonlight was a shiny silver exhaust pipe.

I inched closer. I pulled back the sheet to reveal what-ever was being hidden. I stepped back in disbelief.

Chrome frame. Handlebars. It was a motorcycle.

What on earth was it doing here? Maybe Alexander had bought a Night Rod after admiring the bike outside the club.

But I felt heat emanating from the motorcycle as if it had just been ridden.

I took a long breath and discovered something sweet permeating the air. It was the smell of Obsession.

I sensed a familiar presence standing behind me. I glimpsed down at the floor behind me. A shiny motorcycle boot was blocking me.

I spun around and gasped.

Alexander was looking at me, his soft chocolate eyes staring soulfully into mine. He was wearing a leather motorcycle jacket and pants and holding a purple wig and sunglasses in one hand.

I stood frozen.

My eyes welled up.

"It was you all along." I wiped a tear away from my cheek. "It was you who saved the Coffin Club—and me."

Alexander pulled off his motorcycle gloves and extended his hand, his spider ring almost glowing.

He pulled me into him and wrapped his arms around my waist.

"This is why you had to stay in Hipsterville so long?" I asked. "Not for the art festival but for the Dungeon?"

He nodded.

"But why the disguise?" I asked.

"Jagger and I finally had come to a truce. Not only was

it important to me—but to my family. If he noticed I was in the Dungeon, he would have known that once I'd heard his real intention for the club, I'd try to thwart his plan. I know it sounds strange, but I found it comforting knowing that Jagger and I were no longer nemeses. If I'd shown my face, I'd risk restoring another feud. But someone needed to stop him. And since I couldn't, I had to find someone who could."

I gazed up at Alexander, realizing for the first time why I'd been so drawn to Phoenix.

"It's time to return home, together," he replied, and kissed me with the intensity of two very mysterious vampires. Then he licked his lips and flashed his fangs and grinned. "For eternity."

Acknowledgments

I 'd like to thank the following people for making such a difference in my life and helping make my dreams come true:

My fabulous editor, Katherine Tegen; my awesome agent, Ellen Levine; the terrific Julie Lansky at HarperCollins; my loving parents, Gary and Suzie; my writer-mentor brother Mark, and supportive brother Ben; and my Alexander, Eddie Lerer.

LONGWOOD PUBLIC LIBRARY
Middle Country Road
Middle Island, NY 11953
(631) 924-6400
LIBRARY HOURS

Monday-Friday	9:30 a.m. - 9:00 p.m.
Saturday	9:30 a.m. - 5:00 p.m.
Sunday (Sept-June)	1:00 p.m. - 5:00 p.m.